ULTRAMARINE

JENNY NIMMO

METHUEN CHILDREN'S BOOKS

First published in Great Britain 1990
by Methuen Children's Books
A division of the Octopus Group Ltd
Michelin House, 81 Fulham Road, London SW3 6RB
Copyright © 1990 Jenny Nimmo
Printed in Great Britain by
Redwood Press Limited, Melksham, Wiltshire

British Cataloguing in Publication Data

Nimmo, Jenny, 1942-
Ultramarine
I. Title
823.914

ISBN 0 416 15932 X

ULTRAMARINE

CONTENTS

*For my youngest child
Gwenhwyfar,
with love*

ONE

The Ocean's Footsteps

When Ned reached back for his earliest memory, a dream came to him of being cradled by the sea. This was not so surprising because he had always lived beside the ocean. And yet the dream was something more than the steady throb of the tide and the endless vistas of blue and green and silver. Ned's dream was more a sensation of being carried by infinitely loving waves whose murmur echoed the rhythm of his own heart.

Once he had asked his sister Nell if she shared this dream – this memory. He had hoped her reply would shed light on his dream and that they could unravel the mystery together. But Nell only said, 'Sometimes, I can hear the ocean's footsteps!'

They lived in a row of terraced houses that sat wedged into a cliff above the sea. They were tall, narrow houses, some pink, one blue and several white. The first and last house had a small turret, a glassy half-hexagon with a pointed roof that protruded from the house like the head of a strange crested bird. Their house was one of these.

Leah McQueen kept her precious plants in the turret. Ned longed to have this room for himself but it was without electricity and could only be reached by a small trap-door. Although Leah had replaced the rotting steps with a sturdy wrought-iron spiral staircase, she still thought it an unsuitable bedroom for her son.

When Ned was ten, however, Leah had agreed that he was old enough to prevent his sister from falling through the window, and the children had been allowed to use the turret as a playroom. Yet even now the children did not own the room; they shared it with the ocean that glowered or sparkled in at all three windows. To the south the sea was outlined by the curving finger of Hart's Bluff and to the north by the ragged line of the Belen Cliffs. But the centre window in the turret belonged entirely to the waves and the sky and all the birds that lived there, calling and crying, soaring and swimming their way through the day. And Nell, who loved the birds above anything else, was never happier than when she was perched in the window, watching.

Ned often wondered why his mother had chosen a seaside home for them, for she spent most of her life in steamy dressing-rooms in a town an hour's drive away. She painted other people's faces, powdered actors' noses and combed their hair before they pranced across a billion television screens as someone else. When Ned asked Leah why they didn't live in town she had replied, 'Your father wanted you to live here. He thought you would be happy by the sea.' And, of course, they were.

Every morning Leah would sing herself downstairs, scattering scarves and lipsticks through the kitchen in her search for coffee beans and marmalade, and Ned and Nell would wake to the smell of hot toast and the sound of Leah's accompaniment to Bach or the Beatles. But by the time they had dressed she would always be gone, leaving them only a trace of her flowery scent, an empty cup with ghostly pink lips printed on the rim, and sometimes a note about milk bottles or clean socks.

On stormy days the sea would drown their mother's

10

voice and lull them back to sleep and they would wake too late to brush their teeth or finish their cereal and, even so, miss school Assembly, and have detention for not bringing a note of explanation.

After a while Ned learnt to make an admirable copy of his mother's handwriting, and from her colourful and extravagant language gleaned a repertoire of excuses so outrageous that astounded teachers could only believe and sympathize.

'Dear Miss Noble,

I do apologize for keeping Ned from school this morning. He tells me he should have read in Assembly. What a shame! I had a paralysing pain in my left side. Well, of course, I thought it had to be my heart. Ned had to ring for the doctor and wait by my bed until he arrived. So silly, it turned out to be indigestion. But one can't be too careful. Damn nuisance, actually, because I was to have done Sean Connery! Ah well, *quae nocent docent*!
Yours sincerely,
         Leah McQueen'

The Latin phrases were particularly useful because Ned knew that Miss Noble didn't have Latin.

For Nell, he would make a faithful copy of these letters and substitute her name and her teacher's for his. Once he forgot to change the names and feared discovery, but nothing happened.

Ned enjoyed his literary exercises. He thought they would eventually lead him into being a real writer. He would grow a beard and retreat to a hut somewhere, and there his vocation would be an excuse for uncut hair and irregular clothing. But halfway through this reverie he would remember Nell and know that he would have to delay his retreat until she was launched into a life of her own, and with impossible Nell, what could that be?

Nell was not like other boys' sisters. Ned's friend Thomas Morton had a sister Lucy, who positively avoided her brother, but Nell was different. In the playground she would gradually creep towards him as he played with friends, and he would be aware of her moving in his shadow, watching him as though she needed some contact with him to recharge her batteries and give her the strength to keep going for another two hours.

Nell had been at school for three years now but she still hated it. On reaching home she would cast it off like a heavy cloak that must not even be referred to until necessity forced her to put it on again.

A few weeks before the end of the spring term, Leah was urgently required to meet the Head Teacher. When the children got home that afternoon their mother smiled at them, but the smile came through a cloud that had settled on her. Ned tried to cheer her with his stories and even made some up, but always the little cloud returned until at last he burst out, 'What is it, Mum? What have they said up there?'

Looking towards the open door Leah said softly, 'Your sister's not doing very well, Ned. It's not just her work, they say she seems to be – somewhere else – all the time. What can I do?'

Perhaps if you were at home all day? Ned thought, but that seemed unfair to Leah when her work brought them so many good things. 'If Nell talks about it, tells her thoughts to us, we might find the reason,' Ned said.

'Maybe...'

She seemed to be about to confide; it made Ned want to prod her further. 'Do you know a reason?' he asked. 'Is there something in Nell's past that would make her act this way?' He was thinking of his own dreams of the sea.

'May be,' she repeated thoughtfully but this time with a hint of fear, 'but no it can't be because *you're* all right, aren't you, Ned?'

'Can't be what, Mum?' He searched her face.

She wouldn't say any more on the subject, but all at once she murmured, 'Perhaps a father would help. If I ...'

'No, Mum,' Ned said quickly. 'We don't need a father. I'll sort Nell out, I always do. I can take care of her!'

'Yes, that's true, Ned,' Leah said. 'But all the same you wouldn't mind, would you, if I got married again?'

Ned thought: perhaps it will mean Leah at home for breakfast and teatime, clean football shirts and all the buttons on my anorak. I could manage a father if all those things came true.

Nell knew they'd been discussing her. He could tell. She wouldn't eat her supper. She had a drink of water and chewed on a crust as though it were a penance and then went off to bed without a kiss for Leah.

When she had gone Leah exclaimed, 'You are all right, Ned, aren't you? You're happy, aren't you? Your school reports are good!'

'Of course, I'm happy,' Ned reassured her. 'And school is fine. Why shouldn't I be? Mind you, it would be even better if Dorian was still alive. But being without a father has made me extra-responsible and independent.' He was repeating one of Miss Carter's descriptions of himself, and as if to emphasise his maturity he deftly cleared the plates while Leah sat drumming her long clever fingers on the table.

They could hear the ocean roaring far away, and the roar crescendoed much faster than usual as a flood tide filled the estuary. On the roof excited seabirds screamed about the stranded fish there'd be on the wet morning sand. But their calls were eventually lost in the battle of wind and water. Somewhere a pylon toppled and all the lights went out.

They used the darkness as an excuse to take a candle up to Nell, but she was sitting in the moonlight with a smile on her face. So Leah blew the candle out and they all sat, together, on Nell's bed and talked about the storm. Leah was like that. She'd never tell you to cuddle down and ignore the weather; she enjoyed a night-time chat as much as anyone.

Encouraged by the raging sea, Nell began to talk. Gradually, from her hesitant sentences, they learned that her years at school had been a terrible intrusion on her thoughts. 'I have to concentrate so hard, you see, against all that noise so that I can hear them.'

Leah, suddenly enlightened, cried, 'Nell, darling, can't you hear?'

'Oh, I can hear you and everyone else,' Nell said. 'That's the problem. You blot *them* out. You all make such a noise.'

'Them?' said Ned, intrigued. 'What's *them*?'

'The footsteps,' Nell replied. 'The ocean's footsteps.' And she turned an impatient face to him. 'You know; I know you do!'

Ned watched disappointment draw Leah's face into a frown. She would rather Nell were deaf, he thought, because that's something she can explain to everyone.

Unconcerned by Leah's anxiety, Nell went on, 'When I was little they were just a tiptoe, very faint, so I had to listen hard. Then I discovered that when I came near Ned it was easier, they sort of echoed from inside him, and I felt safe again. I know he doesn't like me to follow him and I try not to, but when I can't hear the footsteps, I think,' she gave a little shuddering

14

sigh, 'I think I'm going to fade away, until I'm nothing.'

'I see,' Leah said, but from her next remark Ned knew that she did not. 'I think that now we've talked about it you'll find those funny footsteps don't matter any more.' She drew a breath and changed the subject. 'Nell, would you mind if I brought a friend home this weekend; a man I've been working with? I'm sure you'll like him and he's very keen to meet you.'

Nell turned to Leah in surprise. 'Is he?' she said. 'I don't mind.'

They sat for a while, the three of them, very close, lit by moonlight and enclosed by the ferocious sea. Was it, perhaps, the last time they would be together in such a way? Ned guessed that whatever Leah believed was her reason for bringing a stranger into their midst, it was really for herself.

He drew himself away from the others and went to the window. A great silver flood had rushed into the estuary, it covered an expanse of land that had never been submerged before. And the tide was still rising. Brilliant, moonlit towers crashed beside the rocks, and the cliff plants, whose survival had always been precarious, began to lose their battle. Clouds of scrub were torn away and hurled over the water. For the first time Ned saw the ocean as a hungry, living thing that could swallow the earth if it had a mind to. Yet the footsteps Nell heard were so gentle that human chatter drowned them. 'They're coming closer,' she whispered, turning to him.

And although he couldn't hear the footsteps he could feel them, ringing through him in time with the thundering sea and building in him such a crazy sort of hopefulness he wanted to shout out loud.

TWO

The Man in a Wave

The morning revealed a tideline of broken furniture, barrels, bags and even a poor dead sheep. The power was still off but the radio announced that it would be restored by midday. It also advised motorists not to undertake long journeys as more gales were expected in the evening.

Undeterred by these reports Leah set off for work, but told the children to stay at home and fetch Aunt Tibby for company.

Aunt Tibby was their next-door neighbour; she'd offered herself as shopper, cook and substitute mother rolled into one cheerful bundle when Leah decided she'd have to go to work again after she had lost her husband. Nell was still a baby then, and Ned at nursery school. It was a perfect arrangement.

Mrs Tibbs had four children who had grown and 'fled her nest'. Her only grandchild was growing up in New Zealand without ever having seen her and she loved children. 'You're mine,' she would exclaim hugging Ned to her motherly bosom. 'You're my true little nephew and niece, aren't you?'

'Well, we're no one else's,' Ned had told her. And this was true. Their father's only sister lived three hundred miles away, his brother had vanished, and their mother's brother didn't care for children much, they'd heard.

'Today we'll have cold ham and salad,' Ned proposed, 'or bread and cheese and chutney followed

16

by ice cream and apples.'

He found that he was already looking forward to the feast he had dreamt up while he was still enjoying breakfast.

'Are you sure we shouldn't be at school?' Nell asked anxiously. 'They won't think we're skiving will they?'

'We won't be the only ones,' Ned comforted. 'I bet some of the school buses won't get through. There'll be trees and stuff all over the roads. It's likely we'll be sent home as soon as we get there; they won't be able to serve hot dinners without electricity.'

Happily reassured Nell asked, 'Could we have chocolate cake as well, I know there is some?'

'Of course,' Ned said.

To while away the morning they made a game of cleaning, timing each other on their rooms and then inspecting for signs of dust, under beds and on top of wardrobes. Then they laid a table for three beside the kitchen window and Ned ran next door to fetch Aunt Tibby. But she was not at home.

Nell was dismayed by the news. 'How long must we wait?' she asked. 'I'm starving!'

'We won't wait,' Ned said. 'She's having a snack in town, I expect. I'll go back at teatime.'

The sky was still dark and brooding so he lit a candle and set it in the centre of the table. The flame lent its sparkle to the glasses and cutlery and Nell's pale face, warmed by candlelight, took on such an entirely peaceful expression, Ned imagined her to be a damsel whose life had been promised to a High Priest, enjoying a final meal before renouncing all good things forever.

Their kitchen wasn't like other peoples'. Leah's machines didn't proclaim their efficiency from well-lit positions of authority, they were placed in discreet corners, disguised with ferns or encased in pine

17

cupboards. Even the sink with its Victorian brass taps was hidden beneath a jungle of trailing plants, and the floorboards had been left free to shout their naked clack-clack when you walked across them.

While the children ate they watched the beach. Clouds of wind-dried sand streamed over the tawny plain that the receding ocean had revealed. The ravenous flood of the night before had vanished, leaving only a trickle at the world's perimeter: a slim line broken in the foreground by tiny feathers of spray. They had never seen the sea retreat so far.

'It's as though it's gone out to fetch something,' Nell remarked, 'and can't find the way back.'

Ned was doubtful. 'More like it's waiting for something,' he said.

'Or someone,' Nell suggested. 'Shall we go out to meet it? Maybe we'll find things no one's ever seen before. Strange fish or special shells.'

'No,' Ned said abruptly. He had a vision of a great wave suddenly rising out of that faraway strip of ocean, as though a monster lurked beneath the gentle surface, waiting to swallow them. 'Besides we'll get sand in our eyes,' he said adopting a sensible tone, 'sand in our hair and our shoes and our mouths. You know what it's like.'

'What shall we do then?' she asked.

'I've got homework,' Ned replied, 'and you know what you've got.'

'Oh, tables,' she remembered with a sigh.

She ran to fetch an exercise book and sat beside the window again.

Ned went up to his room. 'I'll test you at teatime,' he called.

'Shall we finish the cake?' she sang out after him.

'Why not?'

When he came downstairs two hours later Nell

hadn't moved and he was sure she hadn't opened her book. 'It's coming in again,' she said without turning to him. She seemed to find it impossible to draw her gaze away from the sea.

Ned put the kettle on. 'I'll go and see if Aunt Tibby's back,' he said. He ran out into the street and saw for himself, the slowly widening blue-grey band thronged with rearing white horses. Above him soundless leaden clouds rolled toward the ocean, shadowing the beach in a dark blanket. The wind had dropped and a sinister silence stifled the town. Even the seabirds were quiet. They were perched on roofs, cables and rocks in attitudes of watchfulness and apprehension.

Ned flung the ball of his hand against the next-door bell and the ring clamoured into an oppressive emptiness. Again and again he attacked the bell in sudden and unreasonable panic. There was a shuffling noise in the guest house next door and Mrs Elder opened a downstairs window. 'She's away, dear. Just for a night or two. Gone to see her sister. Didn't she tell you?'

'No,' Ned replied, finding it difficult to stop an inner trembling from reaching his voice.

Mrs Elder didn't seem to notice. 'Funny weather,' she observed, extending an upturned hand as though she expected to be instantly rewarded with a fistful of rain. Disappointed, she shook her head and banged the window shut.

'She's out,' Ned told his sister, not even trying to disguise his anxiety this time.

For once, Nell seemed unperturbed. 'Leah will be here soon,' she said. 'Look how fast the tide has come in.'

'I've seen!' Ned didn't want to watch the water. He made tea, then paced the kitchen with a mug in one hand and a biscuit in the other. Finally he left Nell and

19

switched on the television in the sitting-room. He expected her to join him for her favourite programme, but she didn't stir.

She's like those birds, he thought. What's she waiting for? And he wondered if the footsteps she heard had walked out of the ocean at last, and would soon be marching up to their front door. The hopefulness that had so overwhelmed him the previous night had been replaced by fear. If Nell's imagined footsteps became real, perhaps the cradle of his dreams would turn out to be the treacherous arms of a kidnapper.

The television news showed an oil tanker floundering in the heavy seas. The camera was high above it, but suddenly it swung close and a long trail of oil could be seen behind the ship; a dirty carpet on the green water. It was somewhere far away in the Atlantic; Ned barely took in the reasons for the spill, or the danger. He didn't know, then, that the victims would come to mean to much to him.

At six o'clock the telephone rang. It was Leah. 'Darlings, the car's conked out!' She sounded careless and untruthful. 'I'll have to stay put tonight. Get Aunt Tibby over, will you?'

'Aunt Tibby is away,' Ned said, resentment creeping into his voice. 'And I think there's going to be another storm.'

'Oh, Lord,' she exclaimed.

'I expect we'll cope!' He managed to make this sound very unlikely.

'But, darlings, you can't be alone all night. I'll...' Here there was a distant but unmistakable sound of a man's voice. 'I'll get to you somehow,' Leah said. 'Don't worry, Ned!' Over the wires she sounded prickly and it hurt because her face wasn't there to search for those reassuring signs of love.

20

'You don't...' Ned began, but he spoke to a faint click on the line. Leah had gone without even saying 'goodbye'.

Ned had a vision of his mother in her favourite dress, all sequins and not much else, sitting at a candlelit table for two. That's how it would have been, he was sure of it, if Aunt Tibby had been able to take her place. It was the first time Leah had ever done such a thing. But how many more would follow if the owner of that dark background voice became her husband?

If Leah had expected an invitation, been ready to betray them, she would have left the house that morning prepared for the event. He knew he was being possessive and unfair when he went to search her wardrobe. But he couldn't help himself. The red-sequinned dress had gone.

Ned stepped inside the wardrobe. It was easier to talk to an absent mother when you were surrounded by her perfume and her clothes. 'Please come back, soon, Leah,' he said to the soft folds of a grey skirt. 'I'm sorry we spoilt your evening. Come before it's dark or...'

Or what? The rustles of clothes cloaked in polythene reminded him of the sea, and the murmur of the incoming tide crept into his thoughts. 'It'll be too late,' he told Leah's clothes. 'Too late if you come after high tide.'

'What are you doing in there?' Nell was peering into the wardrobe, eyes screwed up for a view into the darkness.

'Looking for a dress,' Ned answered, refusing to be embarrassed. 'I just wanted to know if she'd taken that red shiny thing with her; it's her favourite.'

'Is she staying out tonight?' Nell asked, eyes widening in alarm.

'No. Aunt Tibby is away so she can't. I just wanted to know if she meant to.'

'And did she?'

'Yes,' Ned said brutally, because he wanted Nell to share his anxiety. 'She took the dress with her.'

'Oh!' Nell took herself off as soundlessly as she had appeared so he couldn't tell what she felt.

He found her sitting by the kitchen window again, her chair pulled right round to face the sea now, and her arms folded tight across her chest, each elbow clasped to stop the shivering.

Ned lifted the stove covers, allowing more warmth to penetrate the room. The light suddenly popped on and reminded him of supper. 'Shall we have beans?' he asked. 'Now we've got electricity again.'

'Oh, yes, and lots of hot toast.' There wasn't a hint of uneasiness in Nell's voice. And when she glanced towards him her small face was bright with expectation.

Ned was surprised. It was as if his sister was under some kind of happy spell. 'Leah will be home before dark,' he said, trying to inspire himself with confidence.

'Look at the waves,' she murmured.

Ned came and stood behind her. The sea was tumbling towards the land; a torrent unleashed. The waves were great concave walls, mysteriously black beneath their curves.

He was glad that supper would occupy his attention for an hour and that, after the meal, darkness would give him an excuse to draw the curtains against the sea.

But Nell would not have it. 'Oh let's watch,' she cried, waving forbidding sticky fingers at the window.

Above Hart's Bluff the moon had appeared, huge tonight and with a brightness bursting from it that splashed a brilliant path across the water. Every distant ripple sparkled like a jewel, every wave that crashed against the jetty glittered like a ghostly tower. Their power seemed to take Ned's breath away and he had the sensation of standing on the very brink of life.

'The moon's calling them, isn't she?' Nell said softly.

'Yes,' he answered and, remembering a science lesson, added, 'It's the spring equinox.' And he clutched her shoulder, suddenly, imagining that she too might feel the pull of the moon and soar through the window to join the waves.

'It's the sort of weather that could take your home away, isn't it?' Nell said.

'Not ours,' Ned replied confidently. 'We're too high up.' But a memory stirred, of a house much closer to the sea than theirs, crouching by a tall grey rock. Had he lived there once, and was the sea, at this very moment, pounding at that strange and lonely building?

When they thought that the tide must surely turn and that the ocean had flung its finest battalions at the shore they saw far, far out, a great swell in the water, as though a whale was heaving itself towards the surface. The swell rolled slowly inward, mightier than anything that had gone before it then, slow and tantalizing as magic, a silver crest formed on the long back of the would-be wave, it spilled elegantly forward breaking in a great fountain against the jetty, and to Ned's utter disbelief a shadowy figure began to form in the pinnacle of spray. He thought it had to be a trick of moonlight on water and yet, when the wave had receded the man was there, on the jetty, where there should only have been the swirl of retreating water.

'It can't be,' Ned muttered, desperately rubbing at the mist their breath had made on the windowpane.

'He came from the sea,' Nell whispered.

'It's impossible,' Ned said. 'He can't be human!'

'Neptune!' Nell told him, as though visits from sea gods were an everyday occurrence.

Ned's fierce desire to draw the curtains was arrested by the dark solitary form. Somehow from its attitude he had the impression that the man was looking straight up at them, and that he and Nell and the stranger were united, the only beings in a world that was all ocean.

Before he could recoil from this bewildering sensation, a huge cloud swallowed the moon, obliterating everything. Did the man have night vision to lead him to the shore? Ned wondered. Or would he stumble back into the sea?

There was a sudden and joyfully welcome screech of brakes below and then Leah was climbing out of her little red car, waving and shouting through the wind.

They rushed to meet her and flung themselves into arms full of bright bags and boxes; books for Ned, clothes for Nell.

'You didn't have to,' Ned said as Leah cried, 'Oh, I'm sorry, my darlings, I'm so, so sorry.'

'It doesn't matter,' Nell sang, pirouetting round the kitchen in a black and silver skirt. Something had crept into her and made her sparkle.

Ned added, 'We could have managed, you know. I'm sorry about … about it all.' He didn't mention the car. They all knew perfectly well that the car had not been responsible for Leah's temporary defection.

Later when they sat snuggled together in the big old sofa, and Leah's voice had coaxed them into drowsiness, Ned knew that, somehow, she had returned too late, because the hum of the sea and the spray that glittered on their windowpane were now as comforting as her encircling arm.

'We saw a man in the sea,' he murmured, 'in the biggest wave I've ever seen.'

'You were imagining things,' Leah said. 'No one could swim in water like that.'

'*He* could,' Nell insisted. 'I wonder who he was?'

A distant rumble told them another storm was on its way.

THREE
Enter a New Father

Two days after the highest tide ever recorded Leah brought Mark Howells home.

'Enter a new father,' Ned remarked when he and Nell were alone.

'What do you mean?' his sister asked.

'It's a stage direction,' Ned told her. 'You know, like in a play. Someone different creeps in from the shadowy part at the side and suddenly there he is, in the centre, the hero.'

'He doesn't look like a hero,' Nell observed. 'He's bald.'

They liked Mark, though, they couldn't help it. He was older then Leah and his hairline was definitely receding. He had an attractive, comfortable face with large brown eyes and a smiley mouth. He was clever and dependable and his friendliness was not put on just to please children. He genuinely liked them, Ned could tell. Leah had met him at the Television Studios; they had been working on the same production and the children gathered that their mother's friend was an editor, but had not much idea of what this meant.

Mark spent two whole weekends with them. He introduced Scrabble and Monopoly and long cliff walks. Quiet Sundays with Leah were a thing of the past now.

'D'you think Mark will be our father?' Nell asked Ned during one of their hasty pre-school breakfasts.

'It's obvious,' Ned said loftily. 'Otherwise why all this – communication?' He had forced himself to think of future years with Mark when the few precious hours with Leah would have to be shared.

'At least his children won't bother us,' Nell said. Strange children had always posed a problem for shy Nell. Mark's sons were grown up and had homes of their own.

A week before the Easter holiday Leah and Mark arrived home with good news written on their faces. Years seemed to have fallen away from them and they stood very close, hand in hand, happiness in their voices, and in their eyes a guilty excitement.

Ned watched them almost fearfully. He thought their childish behaviour rather pathetic. He had guessed what they were about to tell him.

They were going to be married! And to complete their happiness they needed the childrens' approval.

Ned wanted to exclaim, 'It's a bit late, isn't it?' But bit it back and said, 'Congratulations,' rather stiffly.

'Oh, Ned, we wanted you to be pleased,' Leah said looking rather hurt.

'I am,' he told her. 'I think it's great. But it's not really a surprise, you know!' He flashed Mark a genuine smile. 'I think I'll tell Nell myself, if you don't mind.'

She was on the floor of her room, bent over an open magazine. A seal lay on a beach; its death beautifully photographed. Below its head a deep indentation spoiled the smooth line of shining fur.

'It's been strangled,' Nell furiously explained. 'You can see the string; it's plastic and it won't break. When the seal was a baby it swam into the string and couldn't get out. It grew and grew until the plastic strangled it!'

'Oh, no!' Ned commiserated. He wasn't sure if Nell was in the right mood for his news.

'We've got to do something. We've got to stop them,' she muttered.

'Who?'

'People. Ships. The sea is full of rubbish and it's killing things.'

'Oh! Well, I know and I agree but, Nell...'

'We'll start right now, shall we? We can take a bin bag on the beach.'

'Nell,' Ned said firmly. 'Leah and Mark are getting married.'

Nell sat back, still frowning at her seal. 'I'm sure she's chosen wisely,' she said.

'That's a funny thing to say!'

'He seems kind,' she said. 'Not the sort of person to take us away from the sea.'

'He wouldn't do that,' Ned agreed. 'Not if he thought it would hurt us.'

'Well it would, wouldn't it?' She gave him a long hard look.

'Come down and tell them you think it's great,' he said. 'You'll see how pleased they'll be. They want us to approve, you know.'

Nell followed him downstairs, her mind on other things. Leah ran and hugged her, pleading for a smile. 'Say you're glad, Nell. We'll all be so happy, won't we?'

Nell mumbled, 'Yes,' while Mark hung a little silver locket round her neck, like a charm to make her his, and then he enfolded his future wife and daughter in a great bear hug.

But the glance Nell directed at her brother, through the weave of loving arms, told him that she did not belong inside this magic circle. She might enjoy their cosy happiness but her heart was still free.

The wedding was sooner than they had expected. Leah must have been very sure of their approval for she had obviously arranged it even before they had met her chosen husband. On Saturday morning at ten o'clock the witnesses arrived: Leah's best friend Marge and her husband Sam. The children liked Marge and Sam, who had visited before and always brought them something. This time it was wooden flutes. They sped off to the Registry Office, Aunt Tibby crammed in between the children. 'We'll have to get a bigger car,' Mark joked.

Nell, disappointed in her desire for a bridesmaid's outfit with lots of lace, was allowed to wear her black and silver skirt and a shiny green blouse. With emerald shoes and a silver ribbon in her hair she resembled some exotic water plant, but ruined the effect by appearing five minutes before the reception with a cardboard placard hung round her neck. 'Smoking Kills' it read in letters that smouldered at one end like fat cigars. Leah tried gentle persuasion, Ned ridicule, to get Nell to remove her gloomy warning, but they were presented with an ultimatum. No placard – no Nell!

'Why not leave it off until after they've cut the cake?' Ned suggested as the first guests arrived.

'They have to know the rules, right from the beginning,' Nell told him patiently.

'That's great coming from someone who hates school,' Ned muttered.

Suddenly the house was full of people from another world, who cooed and chattered and drank quantities of champagne until they giggled on the bubbles and their voices rose or plunged into silliness. The children were introduced to each one but couldn't remember the names that flowed so fast before them. Only three people smoked; they smiled distantly at Nell through their dingy clouds while keeping their gaze carefully above her placard. A man in a plum-coloured suit actually blew clever rings at her. Nell, too shy to voice her disgust, retreated with a silent frown.

'What a darling child,' joked Plum Suit, 'but so serious!'

After the cake was cut everyone decided to take a little jaunt to the beach, leaving Mark and Leah to each other. It was a bright April day; they would dip their toes in the sea and clear their heads for the drive home. Nell pursued the party with a grim expression and a dustbin bag.

'Let's count how many cigarette butts we can find.' Ned hoped to steer his sister clear of the party-goers.

'We'll count *everything*!' she said significantly.

They worked away popping can-rings, bottle-tops, paper and string into Nell's bag until Ned became aware that his sister was deliberately working her way towards Plum Suit who was sprawled on a little mound of pebbles. Suddenly she stopped and said, 'Please put that in the bag!' She pointed to the cigarette butt just out of his reach. 'I saw you throw it.' Her high voice, deadly earnest, rang out above the chatter. Everyone looked at her. Ned was amazed by her boldness.

'Oh leave off, sweetie,' said Plum Suit pleasantly as he lit another cigarette.

Nell glared at him, put her face close to his and said, 'You're polluting our beach and killing yourself, I hope you realize that!'

'Good grief!' cried Plum Suit leaping up. 'I've had enough!'

'She's right, you know, Ronnie,' said Marge laughing at the offended plum back. 'Come on, let's all help!'

And they all did; everyone except Plum-Suit Ronnie, who shambled away from the sea muttering about the tortures he'd like to inflict on some children.

Nell's small brave moment had achieved some-

30

thing. Smart partygoers took off their shoes, rolled up their trousers or peeled off their tights. They pranced across the beach in their silk frocks and best suits, spying, leaping and finding. Nell returned home triumphant, with a bag slung over her shoulder like Father Christmas with a bag of loot.

'It makes you wonder where it all came from,' said Sam, shaking his head. 'I'm afraid a lot of that stuff has been washed in from the sea!'

Nell's smile faded and Ned knew she was thinking of her strangled seal.

Mornings were very different after the wedding. Mark woke his stepchildren with a friendly shout. He was always the first up and busily squeezing oranges, stirring porridge or frying bacon to tempt his new family. And Ned would have to brush his hair before enjoying a wholesome breakfast. Leah hung a large gilt-framed mirror in his room so that he could make sure he looked tidy. She ignored his complaints about 'mirrors looking silly in boys' rooms'.

Beyond the disgruntled reflection in his mirror Ned could see the ocean and he would find himself standing on tiptoe, trying to find a wave that might be carrying a man towards the shore. He often wondered about the misty, impossible figure on the jetty, never doubting that he had seen it.

The children had barely acclimatized to their new life when Leah called them into the kitchen, one afternoon, in the voice they had come to know as her over-cheerful voice, laced with shocks. They left their rooms simultaneously, coming face to face on the landing.

'Something we don't want is going to happen again,' Nell said.

Her brother nodded and they went down

31

cautiously, side by side, united.

Leah was standing in a rather awkward pose behind the kitchen table. Mark was sitting beside her. 'Darlings,' she said, 'I've something to tell you, well ask you, really.'

Mark, sitting within reach of his wife, took one of her hands, in Ned's opinion immediately setting parents and children in opposite corners, as in a boxing-ring. Instinctively, Ned moved closer to Nell. There was no referee, he noted.

'It's about our honeymoon...' Leah waited for a friendly enquiry from her children. It was not forthcoming and so she ploughed on. 'We've been offered this little place in the Algarve, Portugal, you know, a friend of Mark's. It was too good to turn down. I've got ten days' holiday due because of all that overtime I did on *Twelfth Night*, and Mark doesn't have to start on his new production until May – it's all fitted in so marvellously,' Leah accelerated, lost in a rattle of explanations and excuses.

Ned felt numb. He could not bring himself to look at Nell; he could feel dismay radiating from her.

'But it's our holiday,' he burst out, catching Nell's fingers and holding them tight. 'Why can't we come?'

'There's only one bedroom, Ned,' Mark said, looking embarrassed.

'And it's usual for a couple to be, well – alone on honeymoon,' Leah added.

'Who'll look after us?' Nell asked.

'It's all so lucky.' Leah beamed a smile at her children, refusing to acknowledge their dejection. 'Your grandmother can come.'

'We haven't got a grandmother.' Ned was filled with a new foreboding.

'Of course you have.' Leah's smile almost made Ned choke with anger. 'Not my mother, Ned, of course.

32

She died long ago, it's your father's mother.'

A chill little wind blew about Ned's mind bringing a picture of tall grey rocks and the tang of fish. 'With us?' he said. 'She's on an island, all locked up, never goes anywhere, you said.'

'Yes, all locked up,' Nell chimed, as though her words must keep this dangerous relative at bay.

'She's not locked up, Nell, darling! You've got quite the wrong idea. She chose to be a recluse after she'd lost her husband and her son.'

'You said she was strange, and you've only seen her once,' Ned accused. 'How can you leave her with us and on our holiday?' He wouldn't beg, he would force Leah to see the error of her ways.

'Well, in a way you and your grandmother will be caring for each other,' Leah said. 'You remember the spring tide and the gales on the night I...' she flushed and glanced at her husband, 'I got delayed. The islands suffered terribly. Your grandmother's house was swept away, nothing left. Now she's desperate to leave the place; she sounds almost frightened of the sea!'

'Why come here, then?' Ned asked, not unreasonably.

'She has no one else.' Mark came to Leah's rescue. 'Her remaining son seems to have vanished and her daughter lives in a city; all noise and traffic, quite unsuitable for an old lady, who is nearly blind and only used to the sound of the sea.'

'Very unsuitable,' Nell said sympathetically.

'And there's always Aunt Tibby to see to things,' Leah reminded them. 'You know how she loves to be in charge. It's all fitted in perfectly, don't you see?'

No, he would not see. Even in his anger, Ned was searching for a memory beyond his dream of the sea, further and further into the misty places of his babyhood where someone was whispering, 'You bad, bad boy! You'll catch it, yes, you will!' And again he saw the grim grey building crouched against the rock.

'You're selfish,' he cried furiously at Leah. 'We're fed up with coming last in this house,' and he swung away from her, surprised to find he still had Nell's damp hand in his as he marched out of the room.

'Don't be angry,' Nell said as they climbed the stairs.

'*You* are!' he said, ashamed that he wanted her to be angry as well; wanting their doubled anger to swamp Leah and Mark and turn them away from their treacherous intentions.

'It might not be too bad.' Nell eased her hand away from him and sat on the top stair. 'We can spend all day on the beach. She's probably an old woman. She won't be able to stop us.'

'Terrific,' he said. 'Nine days on a beach. No visits anywhere, no museums, no picnics, no Wimpy lunches. I bet Granny McQueen doesn't drive.'

'I don't like Wimpy lunches,' Nell said, gazing at her feet.

'You're being very, very peculiar, d'you know that? You're frightened of being here alone with a strange old granny, you must be. And if only you'd show it Leah might not go. You're the youngest; she'd be afraid of making you unhappy.'

'But I'm not unhappy,' Nell said. 'I'm a bit scared, I suppose, but Leah's in love, she ought to have a honeymoon. And Aunt Tibby will be here if we need her. Besides...' she hesitated, her head on one side, puzzled by her own behaviour.

'Besides what?' Ned prompted.

'Something interesting might happen?' She threw at him such an extraordinary look of anticipation, she might have been another girl altogether.

Ned stumped into his room, and slammed the door.

34

The sea confronted him, frisky and glittering, tossing seabirds playfully from wave to wave. 'You're very jolly today, aren't you!' he said bitterly. 'Sparkle! Sparkle!'

And the sea answered with a message that crept into Ned's soul, securing the little strands of anger that flailed inside him, soothing and comforting, until he was calm.

Later that night, when he was lying sleepless, his light still on, more tired than unhappy, Leah came in and drew a chair beside his bed. He continued to stare at the ceiling, not wanting to discover from her expression whether she was sorry or not.

'Ned,' she said very quietly. 'I'm sorry about the holiday. Please understand. Sometimes you have to grab at happiness before it runs away. You have to forget everything but that, just once, or you're no good to anyone.'

'Happiness doesn't run away!' he grumbled at the ceiling, knowing happiness was another name for Mark. 'Happiness hangs around if it wants to.'

'Ned.' She attempted to find his hand. 'Mark and I have known each other for a year. We've been in love for half of that time but always, always I've put you first. Then, just lately I began to see that Mark and I being together might benefit you, too. You like him, don't you?'

'Yes,' he admitted grudgingly.

'It's only ten days, Ned, and then we'll be back and everything will be just the same, only better.'

Never the same, Ned thought, but I don't mind any more because I know I won't need them much longer.

'Your grandmother sounds very...frail,' Leah was saying. 'I spoke to her on the telephone. She's staying at the Island Post Office, poor thing! I think it will be good for her to be with her grandchildren.'

Ned couldn't help wondering why someone who had hardly seemed to exist had all at once assumed an identity that had become essential to them, or certainly to Leah's happiness. He couldn't bring himself to believe that it was a coincidence. 'Where will she go afterwards; when we don't need her any more?' he asked.

'Oh!' Leah hadn't thought of this. 'I expect her daughter will find somewhere for her. Rhoda's a very busy person. I've written to her but had no reply. She's always on the move.'

'I wonder why the sea drowned two people in our grandmother's family and then took her house away,' Ned murmured.

'You talk as though it were a judgement, Ned. It just happened. Some people have such unhappy lives. Think how lucky we are,' and Leah's own happiness seemed to ebb a little. 'And Dorian wasn't drowned,' she said.

'Tell me, just once more, about the accident,' Ned pleaded, feeling a little guilty that he should do this to Leah on the eve of her honeymoon with another husband. 'I sometimes feel we're losing touch with Dorian,' he explained.

Leah got up and went to the window. She began the little speech she always trotted out after this request. 'It was a terrible night, a seventy-mile-an-hour gale; the road was wet, there'd been a small landfall. Dorian must have braked to avoid it, skidded and – the car went...'

'Into the sea,' Ned finished the unbearable sentence for her, 'and our father drowned.'

'No,' she said impatiently. 'Why d'you always say that. He didn't drown. He died instantly and then, eventually, the car rolled down into that horrible... it's

36

no wonder the locals call it Devil's Mouth; it's a graveyard; rocks that tear at the sea, and water, seething, roaring up at you like something tortured. I went there just the once.'

All at once, from the long sweep of his memory, beyond the clutter of lies and evasions, Ned found the truth. 'But Nell and I didn't drown,' he said.

'No,' she replied, then turned to him, astonished. 'Who told you that you were there!' Her voice came to him like a whisper, taut with fear.

'No one. I've always known it, but you made me forget. Why, Mum?'

'It wouldn't have done any good to know a thing like that. It would have given you nightmares forever. It was a thing to forget.'

She seemed almost angry at his discovery.

Rumble, rumble, rumble. You can hear it now, Ned. You can feel it. You hear the baby screaming. Rumble, rumble, rumble! You're falling, Ned. The stars are tumbling into the sea and it's shining!

'Why didn't we drown, Mum?' he asked. 'With the water all mad and dangerous. We couldn't swim, could we?'

'I don't know, Ned!'

'Is that where I got my scar?' He displayed the mysterious line that ran from his wrist to his elbow. He'd always been told that he'd cut his arm on a broken windowpane when he was three years old, but Leah could never seem to remember which window.

'Yes,' she said quickly. 'That's where you cut yourself.' But he sensed she was lying.

'Why were we there?' he went on. 'Hundreds of miles away in the dark without you? What was happening?'

'I can't tell you any more, not now.' She sounded very tired. 'One day soon, we'll talk about it. But it's not my story. Grandmother McQueen might help you, if she wants to, but don't push too far. It isn't easy after all this time.' She came and kissed him, smoothed his pillow and put out the light. 'You were saved, that's all that matters; delivered on the morning tide; safe on the sand. It was wonderful!'

He liked the picture of babies on the sand. He would add it to the beginning of his store of memories, but there was still a question that wouldn't be silent. Through the darkness he asked quietly, 'Who saved us?'

'I don't know, Ned,' came the reply and even though he couldn't see her face he knew she was telling the truth.

FOUR
Grandmother McQueen

'Couldn't we stay at home today, just to wave goodbye?' Ned asked as they sat, all four, eating an unusual breakfast; a feast of leftovers, beans and ham and apple pie, so that Grandmother McQueen should have a 'fridge full of fresh food, neatly stacked'.

'It's the last day of school, you shouldn't miss it,' Leah said firmly, as she scraped at a sticky saucepan. 'There'll be work to collect; messages from your teachers and your sports kit, Ned, to bring home for washing. Aunt Tibby is going to do the washing by the way, bless her! Grandmother McQueen isn't used to automatics.'

'I wish she could have come yesterday, that grandmother,' Nell said. 'We don't know her and there'll be no one to introduce us.'

'There'll be Aunt Tibby, I'm leaving the key with her,' Leah reminded her. 'If anything should go wrong, there'll always be Tibby, remember.'

Ned sensed desperation in Leah, rising through her carefully constructed happiness. Now that the moment of parting was near he realized that she dreaded it almost as much as they did and was fighting to keep her panic from touching them.

Everyone welcomed Aunt Tibby's cheerful intrusion. She was a small round person with white-blonde curls and an unusually pink and white complexion for the seaside.

'Hullo, my dearies, all packed then?' and without

39

waiting for a reply, 'We'll have a lovely time, won't we, my little mites, without our mum. Just you come and see me if that new gran's not all she's cracked up to be.'

'I don't think she's cracked up to be anything at all,' Nell said.

'Just cracked,' Ned muttered, avoiding Leah's reproving look.

Leah handed the key over. 'Ned's got a key too,' she said. 'I thought he should, just in case.'

'Of course, he's ever such a responsible boy now, aren't we, dearie?' Aunt Tibby caressed Ned's head. 'Take care of my girl, now,' this to Mark along with a smacking kiss. 'You're a lucky girl,' and a kiss for Leah. She talked and moved very speedily for such an overweight person. Every minute of her life was spent getting things done, mostly for other people. They often wondered if she had time to spare for sleep. She swallowed the cup of coffee Leah handed to her, arranged Nell's hair and was gone, humming down the street to her next assignment.

They found they had nothing to say to each other when she had gone and the children left the kitchen to wash and brush until they were tidy enough for the important departure.

When they stood outside the front door Leah embraced them in a hurried desperate way, almost laughing as she kissed them. Mark shook Ned's hand and patted his shoulder, but Nell allowed a kiss and almost seemed to enjoy the hug that followed it. They walked away in step with each other, looked back, just once, to wave and then, without knowing who first decided it, ran all the way down to the High Street where they turned for one more fortifying glimpse of their mother. The door was closed and there was no one on the step.

It was a dark day; a grey mist rolled in from the sea and lay about the shoulders of the cliffs, drifting down, eventually, to wander in salty clouds, along the narrow alleys.

After school Nell and Ned chose to walk home the long way round, very slowly, accompanying Thomas and Lucy to the sea-front where they lived above the stationers. Most of the time Thomas, a chatty person, talked about the holiday he and Lucy were to enjoy next week.

'I wish you could both come too,' he said.

'I wish we could, too,' Ned agreed.

They said their goodbyes and parted rather despondently; Thomas and Lucy disappearing into a shop that blazed with light and bustled with activity. For a moment the McQueens watched the bright window enviously. Their own home when they came within sight of it was a stark contrast to their friends'. They had expected to be greeted by some evidence of their grandmother, but no light showed at the windows. Outside the house, however, a bicycle had been chained to the railings; a high old-fashioned machine painted bright red. Rather dangerous transport for an old woman, Ned thought.

'Let's go to Aunt Tibby,' Nell suggested, staring apprehensively at the dark house, and then at the scarlet bicycle.

But Ned decided that they must tackle Grandmother McQueen head on; they must begin as they meant to continue, unafraid and ready to be loving grandchildren. 'We must go to our grandmother first,' he told Nell, 'we can run next door if ...'

'If what?' asked his sister, her face assuming a fearful and wrinkled expression, in keeping with the old woman she expected to meet.

'If there's no one there,' he said, unable to stem a nervous giggle.

They stood outside their home and Nell said hopefully, 'I thought Aunt Tibby was supposed to be introducing us.'

'That was the idea,' Ned agreed and he stepped up confidently, put his key into the latch and turned. The door swung open on to a dim and deserted hall.

We are not afraid to enter our own home, Ned told himself as he moved uncertainly into the territory that was now shared by a stranger. Nell followed and they stood, with the door open behind them as though reluctant to cut off their escape route. Ned wanted to call out but discovered he didn't know how to address this new relation. 'She'll be in the kitchen,' he said, cheering both of them into a more positive frame of mind. He walked briskly across to the kitchen door, flung it open and stood on the threshold of an unlit room, where two silhouettes rose against the light outside the window.

Nell, close behind Ned, screamed, while a deep but feminine voice said, 'It's the children!'

Ned and Nell stood, unreasonably petrified, as the nearest of the two occupants came towards them. Ned flung his hand, quickly, on to the switch beside him and the hall light blazed into a gaunt and startled face. She was extremely tall, her thick brown hair coiled untidily into her neck, her features defined by the dark hollows under her eyes and cheekbones. She was not pretty but when she smiled, a little diffidently, Ned found her not unattractive. Later he would know that she was beautiful.

'Ned?' the tall stranger said.

'Yes, I'm Ned,' he said and then he found himself asking rather ungraciously, 'Who are you?' She was too young to be a grandmother.

'I am Rhoda,' she replied, and peering round to where Nell had hidden herself in Ned's shadow. 'And is this Nell?'

'Are you supposed to be our grandmother?' Nell asked, ignoring the question.

'Oh, no!' Rhoda's smile broadened. 'I am only an aunt. I came because your grandmother does not ... is not used to children. I felt another hand was called for.'

As Ned made to step into the kitchen his new aunt said, 'Don't put the light on, Ned.' She spoke in a sudden anxious way that deterred him from moving any further.

'Your grandmother's eyes are painful,' Rhoda explained. 'Such a long journey, after so much tragedy.'

'Her house,' Nell ventured, 'was it blown away or ... ?'

'The sea,' Rhoda said quickly. 'The north cliff where she lived just fell into the ocean. They always said it would one day.'

Ned looked, beyond the aunt, into the dim reaches of the kitchen where a motionless figure sat hunched over the table. Was she listening, this faceless old lady? Was she concerned with their voices? Was she even aware of them? 'How did she escape?' he asked, his voice respectfully soft.

'She was hunting in the field behind the house!' Rhoda carefully closed the door on her immobile mother.

'Hunting?' Ned imagined a frail figure striding across the bracken, a rifle slung incongruously across her bony shoulder.

'For eggs,' Rhoda said a little guiltily. 'But she's losing her sight, so her hunts are never successful.'

Why did Ned have an ominous feeling that his aunt was not referring to hens' eggs?

'What happened to her chickens, then?' Nell asked.

'She only had the two bantams, Nell. They flew away, I expect. They're very wild. Shall we go and sit down, children?' The tall woman took their hands and led them gently into the sitting-room. 'You can tell me about your school and what you like to eat, and when we've talked your supper will be ready.'

They found their new aunt a very good listener. Somehow both children managed to convey all they wanted without the verbal scramble for attention they always resorted to when Leah was with them. Rhoda, they felt, would have hours and hours of listening time and would never rush away before she knew everything they needed to tell her. In fact she seemed almost hungry for their stories. And Ned found himself thinking, if only Leah had big spaces in her life that we could fill with all the things we want her to know about us. But he realized that he was being unfair to Leah, who had to go to work because she loved them and wanted them to have all the good things money could buy.

When they had temporarily exhausted their fund of stories, they became aware of a delicious smell drifting across from the kitchen.

'Give me five minutes and you'll have your supper,' their aunt told them, and disappeared.

They stared into each other's expectant faces, counting the seconds breathlessly until Nell said, 'I'm starving!' Then they walked, eagerly but not too hastily, toward the kitchen.

'Come in,' Rhoda called, and they sprang through the door, finding themselves in a cosy kitchen full of light. A vase of golden daffodils had been set in the centre of the table which was covered in Leah's prettiest tablecloth. The grandmother had disappeared, however, and the table had been laid for three.

'Your grandmother eats very little,' Rhoda explained, 'and her diet is different from yours and mine.'

'How, Aunt Rhoda?' Ned asked.

'Please just call me Rhoda,' said his aunt, evading the question. 'I'm not used to being an aunt and I think I would prefer you to think of me as a friend. There, ham pie,' she announced, setting before them a dish they recognized but had never known Leah to cook.

The grandmother might have left them but she was not absent, a hostile presence had been imprinted in the air. Conversation became strained, dwindled to silence. The pie, though, made up for everything. If Ned could have described the effect it had on him, he would have said that the meal satisfied every part of him that was hungry. He had two helpings and, to his surprise, Nell emptied her plate.

'That was great, Rhoda,' Ned said as he scraped a last crumb into his mouth, and he was rewarded with a surprised sort of smile that made him think his aunt was not used to praise.

Their grandmother never appeared. Rhoda accompanied them to their rooms, admired their possessions, tidied the bedcovers and, in Ned's room, found a pile of clothes to wash.

'Aunt Tibby next door is going to do that,' Ned said quickly.

'So she told me,' Rhoda replied, 'but there's really no need. I'm quite used to washing machines, you know.'

'Have you met her? Are you going to be friends?' Nell anxiously inquired from the doorway.

'I think we shall be very good friends,' Rhoda assured here. 'Now, good night, sweet dreams and don't read too long.' She sailed downstairs, retreating

45

quickly and a little shyly from their private night-time ceremonies.

For a long time Ned lay awake, wondering about the old woman in the room beneath his – Leah's room with a window overlooking the sea. And for some reason he felt quite certain that his grandmother was sitting upright, in the dark, sleepless and full of mysterious thoughts.

'How are you going to occupy yourselves?' Rhoda asked next morning.

Ned, who was not used to making decisions at such an early hour, mumbled, 'Dunno,' through a mouthful of toast.

'You could have friends over, if you like, but if you want to go somewhere special, I'm afraid I've only got a bicycle.'

'Oh, it's yours.' Ned remembered the strange red bicycle. 'You didn't ride it all the way here?'

'Goodness, no!' Rhoda laughed. 'I brought it on the train. I wouldn't be without my bicycle. Do you have one?'

'It's too small for me, and Nell won't even try.' He looked at his sister's anxious face and added, 'Well, not yet.'

'Have you friends you'd like to go to?' Rhoda asked.

'We'll be fine,' Ned reassured her. 'We'll go to the beach.'

'Would it be a nuisance for you to show me around a bit?' she asked.

'Oh, of course!' the children answered simultaneously. The beach could wait for a bit. They had ten days to fill and little chance of going anywhere on an old-fashioned lady's bicycle.

'We'll take you on the cliff,' Nell suggested. 'You can see everything from up there.'

When they left the house their grandmother had not

46

appeared. Rhoda made no reference to her and it was not until Nell begged to know if they should see their grandmother at all that day, that Rhoda reluctantly told them, 'I don't know. You see she's tired. I hope you won't be disappointed but you may not see her at all.'

'Not at all?' Nell burst out, running backwards up the steep cliff road.

'Why?' Ned asked.

'She's a little frightened of everything,' Rhoda told him. 'I'm not sure if it was such a good idea, her coming here. She's become very muddled.'

'Poor thing!' Nell cried. The wind snatched her words and threw them to the gulls who echoed her with raucous screams. And Ned was suddenly gripped by the idea that Rhoda, having found the old woman unsuitable as a grandmother, had spirited her away in the night.

'Well, I hope we see her,' Ned said. 'She's the only grandparent we've got.'

His aunt smiled in the enigmatic way that was becoming familiar to them. She pulled her woolly fisherman's hat further down her forehead and began to run up the hill with long heron-like strides, her grey coat flying behind her.

It was the best of days for a view. The sun was low and the distance bright with oncoming rain. From the top of the cliff they could see the cemetery where new gravestones shone, bone-white, beneath a wind-blown yew.

'That's where our dad is,' said Ned pointing.

Rhoda murmured, 'Ah, Dorian. I should like to go there with some flowers.'

'Of course, he was your brother,' Ned exclaimed. 'We don't remember him. You can tell us what he was like. Leah can't seem to explain in the way we'd like her to. We've got photos to show us what he looked like but that's not really enough.'

'Well.' Rhoda frowned intently at a corner of the cemetery, and Ned wondered if she remembered or knew by instinct where her brother was buried. 'Dorian was extraordinary.'

Leah had never told them that. 'D'you mean peculiar?' Nell asked, immediately distancing herself from someone who might not be quite right for a father.

'Oh, no,' Rhoda laughed. 'I mean he was kind and good, and very brave and struggled harder than any man I've ever known to do the right thing. Perhaps the word exceptional is more appropriate.'

Leah had never mentioned any of those traits. She had said that Dorian was clever, a good architect and handsome, and would have been a good father if he'd had the chance. Ned thought that very soon he would tell Rhoda that he knew he had been with Dorian when he plunged into Devil's Mouth and then, perhaps, she would shed some light on that strange day and on Ned's recurring dream of the sea. But he wasn't sure if it was the right moment for Nell to know all this, so asked instead, 'Was Dorian older than you, Rhoda?'

'No,' she answered. 'I was the eldest in the family.'

This was the first time that Ned had ever had a hint that there might be more relations in the world. That Dorian had, perhaps, more brothers and sisters that Leah had never told him about. He decided to keep his questions for another occasion, when he and Rhoda were alone and had time for a long discussion.

They began to wander along the cliff path that sheltered the town and the children took it in turns to name every street below them, and every shop that Rhoda might need for supplies. 'Are you all right for money, Rhoda?' Ned asked suddenly, realizing that Leah had left no instructions as to how their grandmother was to buy food. She had even forgotten pocket money.

'It's all taken care of,' Rhoda assured him. 'I'm a wealthy woman.' She laughed against the wind. 'Don't look so astonished. Some of the richest people in the world travel on antique bicycles.'

'It isn't that,' said Ned, embarrassed. 'We didn't know about you, you see!'

'Did Leah forget you were coming?' Nell asked. 'She's good at that.'

'Leah didn't know,' Rhoda replied, lurching ahead of them.

They followed, in step with each other, and Nell, leaning as close to Ned as she could, whispered, 'Perhaps she isn't a relation at all. Perhaps our grandmother's locked up somewhere, or been sold for a ransom.'

'I don't think I'd mind,' Ned told her. 'I like Rhoda.'

They walked to the end of Hart's Bluff where it cut into the ocean; a square thumb of rock half a mile wide dropping ten metres sheer into a fathom of water. From here they could see the island of Gardeye, once a refuge for monks. The lonely monastery had crumbled away now and the birds had claimed the place.

On the south side of the bluff a rough track led down to the beach and on warm weekends Nell loved to bring Dorian's binoculars to watch the Gardeye guillemots. In spring they would fly in to breed and lay their single eggs on the thin high shelves above the sea; wild dark little birds that lived on the water and never came close. They were Nell's favourite birds.

'Don't go too close,' Rhoda called as Ned stepped up to the edge. He had seen something. One step nearer, against a shout from Rhoda, and he had a full view. It was a sailing boat, the mast broken maybe a metre from the top, and showing pale and jagged. Its white sail was furled along the boom and it looked lonely and desolate riding the empty sea. Perhaps it had been battered by the recent storms, Ned thought. Had its owner been drowned, then? No, for someone had taken the trouble to anchor the boat before abandoning it.

'What are you looking at?' Nell crept closer.

'A boat,' Ned told her. 'Look!'

Rhoda came to his side. 'Broken,' Rhoda remarked.

'It's funny they didn't bring it into the harbour,' Nell said. 'That's where they usually mend things.'

'Perhaps he couldn't!' Ned suggested. 'He anchored as near as he could and then was washed overboard.' Who was this 'he', Ned wondered.

The wind, all at once, threw a flurry of rain into their faces and they retreated.

When they turned, once more, on to the cliff lane Rhoda insisted that Ned and Nell should go home and leave her to shop alone. 'I know where to get the things I need,' she said.

The house was quiet. Not a creak from their grandmother. 'She's here though,' said Nell, 'isn't she? Watching us through the ceilings?'

Ned didn't like to admit it but he felt this too.

When Rhoda came in she carried two bulging supermarket bags and a shiny galvanized bucket. She put the bucket, almost furtively, beside the kitchen door. Curious, Nell went to inspect, and screamed. 'They're alive!' she wailed. 'How could you?'

'Don't be silly,' Rhoda said sharply. 'They're only fish.'

'I don't like fish,' Nell cried angrily. 'At least not to eat.'

'Well, I am surprised, living by the sea, it's surely

just the thing. But as it happens they're not for you,' Rhoda told her. She began opening cupboards, briskly, and with more noise than was necessary. 'Now will someone tell me where the biscuits go!'

Ned pointed to a blue tin on the dresser as he stepped towards the bucket. Four flat plaice shuddered at the bottom. Breathless and frightened their shiny, desperate gaze met his. 'Who is going to kill them?' he asked, horrified by the task ahead.

'Your grandmother will see to it,' Rhoda replied hurriedly. 'Will someone help me to unpack.'

When the shopping had been tidied into cupboards, Rhoda asked Ned to fetch his grandmother. 'Tell her the fish are ready,' she said. 'That will please her!'

Ned ran upstairs, eager to meet this long-lost relation with good news, eager to be welcomed as a wanted grandson. His grandmother's door opened at a touch and she was there, in the doorway, staring out at him with black, hooded eyes.

'Hullo, Grandmother,' Ned said earnestly. 'I'm Ned!'

The look this grey old woman directed at him was not even friendly.

'The fish are ready,' he said, hoping this would squeeze a smile out of her as Rhoda had intimated.

'Good,' she said without warmth. Her voice was surprisingly high and thin, but then she hardly seemed to have a mouth at all, her lips had disappeared into a small fissure beneath her long, bony nose. Her face was untidily scored with deep lines and her coarse grey hair pulled into a tight bun.

She swept past Ned and he followed the surprisingly agile figure down the stairs, thinking this was not a grandmother, this was someone who lurked in horror stories, who lured children into enchanted cottages – and ate them!

Rhoda emerged from the kitchen with Nell behind her. 'This is Nell,' she told her mother.

The old woman stopped on the stairs. Ned could not tell what her expression might be but her high voice creaked as she muttered, 'I can't see much of her. Is she like Ultramarine?'

'Oh, a little, I think.' Rhoda smiled at Nell.

Nell said, 'Hullo, Grandmother. Why should I be like Ultramarine. What is it?'

'I have to kill the fish,' Grandmother coldly informed her. 'You'd better go away.'

Rhoda intercepted the hurt frown Nell directed at her brother, and took her into the living-room. Ned, sidling into the kitchen, followed the grey figure to the sink. The fish had been placed in a bowl of fresh water, where they flipped disconsolately in chlorine. A long kitchen knife had been laid, neatly, on the bare draining board. Ned's grandmother grasped the knife in her right hand while she barked, 'Go away!'

Ned did not move. Horrified by this ritual, he stood spellbound at her shoulder.

'I've told you once,' she hissed, raising the knife, 'so be warned!' And she plunged the knife down into the bowl. Blood streamed from the white belly of a fish and Ned left the room. 'She shouldn't do that,' he told Rhoda. 'It's horrible!'

'It's her way,' said his aunt. 'When you live on an island you have to.'

'I'll never eat fish again,' Ned muttered.

'Nor me,' Nell agreed. 'Not even fingers.'

'But you must have seen the fishermen kill,' Rhoda protested. 'It's surely not so very dreadful.'

'That's different,' Ned said sullenly. 'It isn't the same as murdering something in your own home. And anyway we never looked, did we?' He turned to Nell, who silently shook her head.

52

Their grandmother took her meal upstairs. She did not even want to share a room with them it seemed.

'I get the distinct impression that our grandmother doesn't like us,' Ned said gloomily munching sausages. Nell grimaced at her plate and he wished he hadn't spoken.

'Give her time,' Rhoda said. 'She's never lived on the mainland. Being fixed to a great land mass is a shock to her, she's a long way from home and she doesn't feel safe. She's just a bewildered old lady who needs a few days to adjust.'

Angry old lady, more like, Ned thought. 'I thought she wanted to see us,' he said. 'If you hadn't come, too, we'd have starved or had to eat live fish.'

'There was no danger,' Rhoda said. 'I always keep in touch.'

'We didn't know anything about you...' Nell began.

'Except for the presents,' Ned said quickly, for he had suddenly remembered something. 'There was a boat and a kite...'

'And a wooden cat and a patchwork doll,' cried Nell. 'You are Arntar!' Not being a reader she had always used this slightly exotic name to describe the aunt who, she was told, signed herself, 'Aunt R.'

'Yes,' said Rhoda laughing. 'But now, please, I am Rhoda.' And her smile made Ned resolve that soon he must unravel the mystery of this rather beautiful aunt's absence from their lives.

'We'll go on the beach now,' Ned told Rhoda when the clean saucepans and crockery had been stacked in all the right places. 'What will you do?'

'I? Oh, I shall wander this lovely house for a bit,' his aunt replied, happy and somehow surprised by the question, as though no one had ever asked her such a thing. 'I shall rediscover you,' she went on, 'as I tidy your possessions. And then I shall take my bike for an airing.'

She waved to them from the kitchen window and they noticed that, in the room above, the curtains were closed.

'Why does our grandmother sit in the dark?' Nell asked.

'Perhaps she lived in a thunder-cloud,' Ned replied, trying to sound lighthearted. He hated to think of the old woman casting gloom over Leah's bright room, eating dead fish!

The sea was very quiet. They couldn't see the horizon. A thick mist hung over the water and, in the distance, a mournful foghorn could be heard. There were several other children on the beach, one of them was Tracy, a girl in Nell's class.

'Why don't you go and play with Tracy?' Ned asked. 'I don't mind.'

Nell wouldn't leave him. He despaired of her shyness but knew it would be hopeless to force her away from him. They drew huge shapes in the sand, then letters in a game that Ned gradually eased into a spelling lesson. Nell began to enjoy herself. She was excited by her achievements; recognizing letters, putting them together, finding her name and Leah's. And, as Ned worked, running backwards while his heel dug into the damp sand, he was all the time aware that someone was approaching them; an undefined image drifted at the edge of the sea, its contours gradually resolving into a tall figure that moved through the water almost in rhythm with the waves. He was very tanned and wore only a tee shirt and jeans. His feet were bare and his shoes, tied together with string, hung round his neck.

It was only when he had taken in all the stranger's features that Ned began to write his most ambitious word. The letters slipped, unbidden, into his head and slid through to his feet like poetry. For a moment Ned thought the stranger was inventing the word and passing it to him like a spell, for it seemed that every syllable matched a measure of the man's easy strides through the water; he even slowed his pace a little to allow Ned to keep up with him, while Nell danced round and round, chanting each sound she found, over and over, yet unable to join it all together.

At last the completed name came singing out of the sand, each letter as even and beautiful as though drawn by magic. It was the word their grandmother had used. Ultramarine!

FIVE

In the Turret

The man stopped moving and Nell stared at the word in dismay, searching for a way to make sense of it. 'I can't,' she wailed. 'It's too long!' A little wave swept round her and seeped into each letter. The tide had turned.

The man moved closer. He stood behind Nell and the sea brushed their legs with silvery spray. A watery film trickled across Ned's word and stole some of it back to sea. The man said, 'Ultramarine!' as though the word belonged to him and had accidentally fallen on to the sand.

'You've spoilt it,' Ned cried. 'She was supposed to guess!'

'I never would have,' Nell said, turning to look up at the stranger. 'And now it's all going out to sea!' She seemed delighted at the man's appearance. Whether it was because he had helped her in her work or because he was unusual, Ned couldn't tell. He had a mane of tangled bronze hair, a neat beard and startling sea-green eyes.

'Why did you write that word?' he asked Ned.

It would have sounded silly to say, 'Because you meant me to,' and so Ned murmured, 'I don't know. I suppose it was a test. Nell finds spelling difficult, you see.' He glanced away from Nell's reproachful glare and added, 'But then she's only eight!'

'Perhaps it would be fair, if I gave you a test as well,' the stranger said; his voice was rich and musical and there was an accent in it that Ned could not identify.

'All right. My name is Ned, and this is Nell!'

'And have you always had those names?'

'I think so,' Ned replied, surprised.

'They call me Arion,' the man told them. 'Shall we go closer to the shore where the sea won't steal our words too soon!' He took Nell's hand and she willingly allowed him to lead her across the sand.

Ned followed, worrying that he shouldn't have allowed a stranger so easily into their game, and wondering what he should do about it. 'Is it *Mr* Arion?' he asked.

'Arion will do,' the man answered unhelpfully. Releasing Nell he drew his heel across the sand and soon the word 'Dolphin' appeared.

Ned sang out the name adding, 'That was easy!' He began to relax. There were people on the beach. The man could not kidnap them.

'Now one for Nell,' said Arion and wrote, 'Fish,' which she immediately recognized.

'I want difficult ones, too,' Nell said.

There followed the words 'Brine' and 'Buoyant' and 'Cetacean'.

'What does that mean?' asked Ned, referring to the last word.

'A sea mammal, Ned,' he was told. 'A whale – a dolphin!'

'I love them,' Nell cried, hopping round Arion's words. 'I love them because they've got the sea in them. I'd read them if those words were in my books.'

'Here's something different, then.' Arion glanced at them in a meaningful way that made Ned wonder if the next word was going to hold a message for them. The letters were formed with infinite care and when Arion had finished he stood beside it like a tall exclamation mark. His sea-green eyes bore into Ned's expectantly.

'Albatross,' Ned read aloud. 'That's a bird, isn't it?'

'The most truly marine of all seabirds,' Arion told him. 'They live on the wind and sleep in the sky. Their wingspan is more than two metres. They could circle the globe without stopping if they wanted to and they only follow man by choice, owing him nothing. They are truly free.'

Ned didn't know what to make of the man's hopeful expression. He felt that something more was expected of him. 'They sound great,' he said awkwardly. 'My sister knows more about birds than I do!'

Nell had come to rest beside them. 'One for me before the sand is covered altogether,' she begged.

This time Arion swooped across the beach in loops and strides, while Nell danced after him, slowly singing, 'R – ai – n – bow! Rainbow! Rainbow! It's my favourite word.' Nell who was shy of her own friends was as easy with this stranger as if she had known him all her life. And all at once Ned realized that Arion was not quite a stranger. They had seen him before, riding an impossible wave on that stormy night and gazing at them from the jetty as though he and they belonged together.

The sea came tumbling round them and all their words were hidden. They stood in the waves and laughed as the water rose higher, threatening to fill the children's wellingtons, and as they retreated up the stone shingle, Arion asked, 'Would you know where a weary mariner might rest for a while?'

'You're shipwrecked, aren't you?' Ned answered with a question.

Arion smiled. 'Perhaps we should say temporarily grounded,' he said.

'You can stay with us,' Nell cried, not giving Ned a

chance to disagree. 'There's an attic at the top of our house. It's all windows and our mother uses it for flowers, but I'm in charge of watering and no one else goes up there. There isn't a bed or any furniture but lots and lots of cushions, and we could bring blankets and food!'

'Our mother is away,' Ned explained nervously. 'And our grandmother might not agree!'

'But it's quite secret in the turret,' Nell broke in, 'she'll never know.'

'Yes, but...' Ned wrestled furiously with his doubts. He knew he should not let an unknown man into their home and yet he wanted to. Leah should not have left him to make these impossible decisions.

'I'm not a fugitive,' Arion said gently, 'and quite prepared to be revealed to your relations, though I suppose I am not as presentable as some would like.'

'It's not that,' Ned said. 'It's just that we don't know our grandmother very well.'

Sensing Ned's dilemma Arion said, 'Perhaps it would be better if I went elsewhere.'

Ned thought of Aunt Tibby who put herself at risk all summer with unknown paying guests, and when he looked into Arion's face he knew very well that they would be safe with him. 'No,' he said emphatically. 'You can stay with us. We'll say you're an uncle if they find you. They won't know, you see, because they've never seen us until yesterday.' He led the way up the stone steps from the beach, feeling pleased and proud of his decision. 'They don't know anything about our lives,' he added scornfully.

'How interesting,' Arion remarked, 'to have a dose of two strange relations all at once. I hope they're to your taste.'

'Terrible,' Nell groaned dramatically.

'Not both,' Ned protested. 'Our aunt's all right. Are

you always at sea, Arion? I mean, what is your work? Are you a traveller or a fisherman or what?' He felt duty-bound to make a few more inquiries, though he had already decided that if Arion admitted to being a smuggler or a merman it wouldn't make any difference.

They were standing, all three, on the promenade now and Arion, glancing out to sea, said, 'My world is the sea, my life that of rescuing.'

It was a strange answer, yet Nell found it was exactly what she wanted. 'You're a life-saver,' she said happily.

Arion nodded slowly and Ned asked, 'Do you use your boat then, to answer distress signals? Is it a lifeboat with a horn and lights and all the stuff you need to save people?'

'I save creatures, Ned, not men!' Arion said fiercely.

Somewhat shaken by Arion's savage response Ned fell silent and it was Nell who guided the stranger through the town's narrow streets.

'In the summer holidays there are so many people here you can hardly pass on the pavement,' Nell told their new friend. 'And you don't notice the gulls or the boat sheets rattling in the wind, because there's chatter and shouting and traffic everywhere.'

'Then I'm glad I chose the spring,' Arion said.

'Did you choose it?' Ned inquired, thinking of the boat with the broken mast.

'Perhaps it chose me,' Arion replied. His smile was so warm it made Ned feel very special, almost as though they shared a secret.

They had reached the beginning of the road that wound away from the town up to the terraced houses that ended in their home. And Ned began to worry about all the windows they would have to pass, where idle landladies spent off-peak seasons overlooking their neighbours' activities. And yet, how were they to know that Arion was not a long-lost uncle home from the sea; in which case Ned was proud to be seen in his company. Even in jeans Arion was grand, somehow; his head held as though braced for a storm, his bronze beard completing the defiant thrust of his jaw. And Ned wished that it could be Dorian, their lost father, whom they were leading home forever. But Dorian was buried in the windy cemetery at the other end of town. And when they took flowers to him their mother's cheeks would be stained with dark streams, and they could never be sure if it was sadness or the wind that caused them.

So this new companion could not be Dorian, or even Dorian's ghost, but it was not impossible that he could be someone related to them, for they had been drawn together by something more powerful than casual interest or coincidence. Ned felt certain that it was not chance that had brought this stranger striding up the hill beside them but an infinitely mysterious connection.

The road angled as it approached their house then dwindled towards the sea into a track that led to the clifftop.

The curtains were still drawn in Leah's bedroom but Ned fancied they shivered a little when they got closer and the light behind them altered imperceptibly. Had Grandmother McQueen seen them, he wondered?

The bicycle was not chained to the railing so Rhoda was still out. Ned opened the front door and motioned Arion to follow. They removed their wellingtons and, once again, Arion threaded his shoes together and hung them round his neck. The narrow hall all at once seemed to shrink around him; though he was not so broad or as tall as some of their visitors, he had to stoop to avoid Leah's beaded lampshade. Ned decided it must be a way Arion had of capturing everything in a fierce glance and, somehow, altering it to suit himself.

Nell led the way upstairs, pausing on the landing to put a finger to her lips, then pointing to the closed door that hid their grandmother. At this Arion smiled so broadly, Ned was sure a sound must burst from him. But he obediently followed Nell to the second staircase and his bare feet made hardly a sound on their elderly floorboards.

'Here are more rooms,' Nell said. 'A tiny bathroom, which can be yours, and these are our bedrooms.' She indicated two doors, one either side of the wrought-iron scarlet steps that spiralled to a trap-door. 'But this is where you'll be,' and she could not help the bright spark of gladness that shook in her voice as she climbed to the trap-door.

Ned experienced an unfamiliar light-headedness as he stepped after them. He felt that he was following a pre-ordained pattern. They were not harbouring a stranger but recapturing a strayed and precious possession. He emerged into the room where Nell and Arion stood looking out at the sea. Around them Leah's polished windows burned with sunlit reflections of plants and toys and scarlet cushions: an undersea kingdom glowing in a turquoise sky.

'You seem to belong here,' Ned said quietly.

'It's as fine a crow's nest as a mariner could want,' Arion declared. 'I'm the most fortunate man in the world to have found it,' and he added in a strangely wistful tone, 'and you!'

He took their hands and Ned felt that he and Nell and the stranger formed a charm that could not be broken. All three were on the brink of a voyage of discovery and adventure. He did not even consider the possibility of trouble or disappointment.

'Electricity doesn't come up here,' Nell said, as though it were a creature whose habits did not include lighting glassy turrets. 'You'll have to have a candle.'

'Even candles are a luxury,' Arion said in an undertone. 'I'm used to starlight.'

Ned suddenly spied a familiar figure on a red bicycle. 'Rhoda's coming,' he exclaimed, drawing his companions out of her sight. 'We'd better go, but we'll bring you some supper and a candle to see it by.'

'I should be glad of that,' Arion said.

As he closed the trap-door behind him, Ned's last view was of a pair of exceptionally fine feet, tanned and as smooth as a polished statue.

For supper Rhoda produced a casserole that she had left cooking slowly in the oven. It was another delicious recipe that Leah had never quite got the hang of. Grandmother McQueen ate only one meal a day, their aunt told them. The children glanced at each other over the steaming dish, relieved to hear that no more fish would be murdered that night.

At a silent request from Ned, Nell took Rhoda into the living-room as soon as supper was over. 'Will you watch television with me?' she artfully requested. 'Ned won't and I don't like watching on my own.'

Rhoda agreed, never guessing Nell's motive. When the living-room door was safely closed, Ned ran to the drawer where Leah kept her candles. He stuffed a candle and a box of matches into his pocket, then scraped the remains of the casserole into a bowl, cut a fat slice of bread and went upstairs. He had just reached the first landing when his grandmother's door was jerked open and she stood glaring at him.

'I'm just having a second helping in my room,' he explained, holding the bowl awkwardly against his chest.

She wasn't interested. 'Where's the girl?' she asked.

'Nell? She's watching television.' Ned breathed more easily.

'Television,' she sneered. 'D'you watch it, boy?'

'Sometimes!' Was she keeping him here on purpose, Ned wondered, so that he shouldn't enjoy the cooled casserole. 'Not much, though,' he amended. 'I like nature programmes.'

'Never seen them,' she said. 'Nature. I keep away from it.'

'How could you on a wild island?' Ned asked, amazed yet stepping closer. 'It must have been wonderful. All those birds, and Leah told us you could see seals and dolphins, sometimes.' He had hoped that, one day, his grandmother might describe her island to him.

The mysterious old woman put her head on one side, stretched out her long neck and peered into his eyes. 'You keep away from it,' she warned, 'or you'll turn funny.'

Unable to reply Ned stared at the scrawled map of her face and found, in the furtive dark eyes his own reflected panic. He felt an irresistible urge to touch her so that both of them should be unafraid. 'It's all right, Grandmother,' he said gently. 'I won't turn funny.'

She recoiled, stepping behind her door and peering round it at him. 'I know what you're up to,' she muttered and closed the door.

Ned felt such a chill strike through him he almost dropped the bowl. Either his grandmother had guessed they had a visitor, or she was trying to frighten him for some mad reason of her own. Nervous and unsteady he crept up the second staircase and on to the spiral. The winding steps were more difficult to negotiate for he had to hold the rail and then use a free hand to open the trap-door. But the door swung open just before his head touched it. He handed the bowl up to Arion and, scrambling quickly into the turret, closed the door noiselessly behind him.

'I'm sorry,' Ned whispered. 'The food will be cold. My grandmother kept me.'

'I heard,' Arion quietly replied. 'The food looks very good.'

Ned brought out the candle, lit it and set it in an empty flower pot. Above the reflected candle-glow he could see his own shocked face staring at him from the uncurtained window and said huskily, 'She said she knew what I was up to. Either she knows someone is here, or – she's a bit mad.'

'Both perhaps,' Arion suggested and when Ned turned to him, more frightened than surprised, he added, 'but probably neither.' His strong face looked so calm Ned felt his unease recede until he began to wonder why an old woman had caused such a turmoil in him. He was all at once supremely happy, as though all the aching corners in his life had been soothed by invisible waves, and he was reminded of his dreams. If he had been asleep, he thought, he would be dreaming of the sea. He had an urgent desire to tell Arion all this but did not know how to convey such sentimental thoughts to an adventurer who would, in all likelihood, regard the ocean as challenging and dangerous. But at length and in spite of himself, Ned found himself saying, 'Once, when my sister and I were very small, we fell into the sea. We should have drowned but we didn't. The sea saved us; and ever since then, especially when I'm sad, I dream about being rocked by water, just like in a cradle, and it makes me feel very safe. D'you think that's crazy?'

Arion's face had taken on such a puzzling and intense expression, Ned had the impression that he was controlling an urge to make a violent gesture of some sort, but instead he placed his bowl, very carefully, on the floor beside him, put his hands together and brought the tips of his fingers to his lips. For several seconds he stared at Ned over his hands and Ned couldn't move; he was mesmerized by the leaping candle-light in the deep-sea eyes and recalled how the frosty stars had repeated themselves in the dark water that awaited him on the day he fell into the sea.

'Are you often sad?' Arion said at last.

'Oh, no,' Ned fervently assured him. 'I suppose I used to be a bit worried because I couldn't understand my dream but recently I've heard that we were in the car with my father when he crashed and drowned, well, not actually drowned. My mother says he died from knocking his head, really. So I suppose it would make sense, all those sea dreams. But there's still part of it she won't explain. She says my grandmother might tell me; but I can't imagine that happening now.'

The man opposite him had remained motionless while Ned talked and, in a sudden fear that all the calm safety Arion represented did not really exist, Ned put out his hand to make sure the man was real. The hand was taken and held in a firm grasp that had nothing ghostly about it, and Arion said, 'Tomorrow, I will bring you something!'

Before Ned could reply there was a shout from below, 'Ned, are you up there?' Ned froze; he realized he had been away for longer than he'd intended. Rhoda might come to investigate. 'It's my aunt,' he whispered.

'Just call back to her,' Arion said softly. 'There's nothing to worry about, no reason why you shouldn't be in a favourite room, though perhaps the appearance of a stranger at such a late hour would be a little frightening to her.'

'I'm here,' Ned called, opening the trap-door as he spoke. 'I – I was just seeing to the plants for Leah. We forgot earlier.' He began to descend the spiral staircase.

'Oh, I see.' Rhoda's voice was easy and unconcerned.

Ned smiled at the man and gave a silent thumbs-up sign. Arion handed him the empty bowl and closed the trap-door.

Rhoda and Nell were in the living-room. The television had been turned off and Nell was tucked neatly into an armchair. She looked like a small sleeping animal.

'She seems to be rather tired,' Rhoda said, looking at Ned over the top of her reading glasses; the huge round frames softened her features, giving her an altogether more relaxed appearance. 'Do you want to watch television, Ned?' she asked. 'Or have you got homework?'

'I'm entering a writing competition,' he admitted. 'Can I do a bit in here?' The living-room seemed safer than the kitchen. It was crammed with snacks that might tempt a sleepless old woman into an evening excursion.

'Of course.' Rhoda made room for him on the sofa.

'I'll do it on the table by the window,' he told her. 'Have you noticed that you can see the ocean from every room in our house?'

'I have. It reminds me of home. I live so far from the sea now; I miss it!' She smiled and returned to the world in her fat paperback.

Ned fetched his schoolbag from the hall. He opened his exercise book on the round table and then looked out at the sea, granite grey under the dusky clouds. He thought happily of Arion in the turret, perhaps sharing his view. Turning to his book he began to invent a story. When he looked up again Rhoda was leading Nell out of the room.

'Are you going to bed, Nell?' He turned round in his chair.

'Yes,' she yawned.

For a moment the room was tranquil and secure and then Rhoda asked, 'May I visit your hideaway tomorrow, Ned?'

'Hideaway?' he asked, bemused.

'Your turret. I should like to see the plants.'

'No!' Nell cried, springing to life, fists clenched. 'It's our room; our secret room. You're not to go there, ever!'

'I'm sorry.' Rhoda stepped back. 'I didn't mean...'

'We'll show you,' Ned hastily broke in, 'one day. But not now if you don't mind.'

'Of course I don't mind,' Rhoda said with a frown. 'I know you must have some secrets. I realize that.'

'Yes,' Ned agreed. 'But we'll let you see it, one day, won't we, Nell?'

She looked back at him, fierce and unrepentant. 'Maybe,' she said, then, relenting a little, 'Good night, Rhoda!'

'She can't help it,' Ned told Rhoda when his sister had gone. 'She gets like that sometimes. She doesn't mean anything by it.'

'It doesn't matter, Ned. I'm still a stranger,' Rhoda said, as though it were she who should be apologizing for her intrusion into their lives. She removed her glasses and, folding them carefully, asked, 'Would you like a drink?'

He nodded vigorously. 'Cocoa, please, with loads of sugar!' He gave a guilty grin. 'I'm trying to give it up.'

'Cocoa needs sweetening,' she said.

When she brought Ned his cocoa she carried a mug for herself, which she began to sip as she resumed her reading. It might have been a routine they'd been following for years, their silence was so peaceful and friendly. Half an hour later Ned left the room with a murmured, 'Good night,' which Rhoda acknowledged with a faraway, 'Sleep well, Ned.'

Rhoda is a good person, he thought, and it occurred to him that she might hold the answer to his mystery, in which case there should be no difficulty in getting at the truth. He tiptoed back to the living-room and asked shyly, 'Could we talk about Dorian tomorrow?'

She gave him a delighted smile and said, 'Yes, Ned. I'd like to do that!'

He was already drowsy when he climbed into bed, but tried to keep awake in order to recapture the day's events; he wanted to sort everything out, chronologically, because he knew that it all fitted together in a way that he could not yet explain to himself.

In the middle of the night something woke Ned up. For a moment he couldn't imagine why he was awake. And then he became aware that the sea was in the house, and his bed was floating. He allowed himself to be rocked, very gently, just as he did in his dreams, only he knew that he wasn't asleep this time, because he could feel his heart beating and, above his breathing, hear the steady slow rhythm of the waves.

The room was full of a soft light that came from tiny threads of glowing silver that rippled over the ceiling, and Ned told himself that he was looking up, from a great depth, to the surface of a sea patterned with moonlight.

He lay enjoying this sensation, puzzled but without any fear, until a scream echoed through the house. The canopy of shining waves burst above him, and his bed was fixed to the floor by an invisible rock that seemed to have hurtled through the water above him. All light vanished and Ned struggled for breath, like a fish deprived of water.

SIX

'You're not our grandmother.
You're a witch!'

A voice below continued its ragged shrieking and Ned tumbled off his bed, pulled himself to his feet and lurched to the door. He came face to face with Nell.

The scream was dwindling now to a toneless moaning and, peering over the banisters they saw their grandmother, in a white nightgown, her long smoky hair covering her shoulders like an untidy shawl. 'It was here!' she suddenly shrieked. 'I heard it; my bones recognised it. You let it in, Rhoda!'

'Hush!' Rhoda, in a blue dressing-gown, made soothing sounds as she held her mother's hands, saying over and over, 'Mamma, Mamma! It's all gone now. You were dreaming!'

'Liar!' yelled her mother. 'Traitor. What do you know? The ocean was in this house. It won't give me any peace!' Her voice rose to an unnatural screech.

'The children,' Rhoda reminded her in a soft and urgent voice. 'You'll wake them.'

'They'll know if they're who they are. They brought it here most likely,' said the old woman, this time low and venomous.

Rhoda put an arm about her mother's shoulders and began to urge her to her door, but before they were out of sight, Nell gave a confined little sneeze and her aunt looked up. 'Children,' she said with surprise, 'I'm sorry we woke you. Your poor grandmother still has bad dreams about the sea!'

70

Niece and nephew stared down at her, both disbelieving because they knew the sea had swept into their house; they knew they had not been dreaming.

'Good night, then,' Rhoda said uneasily as she steered her mother back into her room and closed the door.

'Did you see it?' Ned whispered.

'I heard it,' Nell replied. 'I heard the ocean's footsteps walking all around me, very, very close. It was like dancing, almost, or singing – music anyway. I wanted it to go on forever. And then that awful noise began, just before the front door banged.'

'The door? Are you sure it was the front door?' Ned asked.

'I think so! Ned, what did our grandmother mean? Why did she say that about us being who we are? What are we?'

Ned dolefully shook his head. 'I wish I knew. We'll ask Rhoda tomorrow. Better get some sleep now.'

As they turned to go into their rooms they paused, surprised to find moonlight spilling on to the landing. They looked up and saw the open trap-door.

'He's gone,' Nell remarked sadly. 'That screaming drove him away.'

'Perhaps,' said her brother. But as he rolled himself back into bed, Ned wondered if it hadn't been the other way about. Could Arion's footsteps have caused the scream?

'Good morning, everyone.' Ned sauntered rather self-consciously into the kitchen. He had overslept and felt sheepish about it.

Nell was hunched over cornflakes as though held there by an unseen weight. Rhoda, sitting opposite, looked ill at ease.

The memory of their grandmother's screams lay

71

over the room, even reaching the sky outside, which was swollen with rain.

'Is Grandmother all right, now?' Ned forced himself to ask.

'More herself, thank you, Ned,' Rhoda replied, awkwardly polite. 'I don't think she knew who you were last night. She was very bewildered.' They left the subject of the night's disturbance and made strained remarks about the weather.

When Rhoda took a cup of tea to her mother Nell leant close to Ned and said, 'I've got something to show you.'

He followed her out to the hall where she pointed to the stairs. On every step, where the carpet folded, there was a small pocket of sand. They followed the sand, like a treasure trail and found, at the base of the newel post on the first landing, a pile of tiny shells.

'They're so beautiful,' Nell whispered, for they were now almost directly outside the room where their two relations murmured to each other behind the closed door. 'I've never seen shells like this on our beach.'

Ned picked one up. It glistened in his hand, like a polished jewel.

'The ocean brought them,' Nell said. She looked intently into his face and added, defiantly, 'It did!'

'Perhaps they came from Arion,' he said. 'He probably carries them in his pockets, or even in his hair. He's at sea, or on beaches all his life, so they become part of him, like we carry dust mites.'

'There are more,' Nell pointed to a glistening sprinkle beside Rhoda's door. 'And on the next landing, under the spiral staircase, there are little pieces of seaweed and more shells. It's like an enormous wave, bigger than the one that brought the man, whooshed into our house and out again, leaving all these treasures for us. Our grandmother wasn't dreaming.'

'No,' Ned agreed, and as he turned to walk downstairs he saw clearly, on every step, a large wet footprint. He hadn't noticed them on their way up because the light on the carpet pile disguised them, but now, glancing down the long sweep of stairway each footprint could be clearly discerned; left, right, left, right, as they descended. Perhaps the left was clearer than the right, which was more rounded and did not appear to have any toes.

'The ocean's footprints,' Nell remarked with awe.

Their grandmother's door opened and she appeared, as though from a nightmare. Her hair had been swept into a disorderly plait around her head and her hostile glare transfixed them.

'Get me some fish,' she demanded of Nell.

Nell's mouth dropped open. 'She can't,' Ned objected. 'It's not her job.'

'Mother, don't!' Rhoda was in the doorway now. She put a restraining hand on her mother's arm.

'Do as I say.' The old woman pulled away from Rhoda and wouldn't look at Ned. It was Nell she was after. 'The boats are in. I need a fish and my daughter must stay with me today.'

'No,' Nell cried, alert with horror. 'You'll murder it and that's not allowed in our house. You're wicked!'

Faster than anyone could have imagined, Grandmother McQueen sped towards Nell and brought her hand smacking against her cheek. Nell reeled back and clutched the banister. Ned saw her newly acquired glow of confidence begin to dim, leaving her small face so drained of life, he thought she would collapse. But with a superhuman effort she screamed, 'You're not our grandmother! You're a witch!' and she flung herself down the stairs.

Before he leapt after his sister, Ned noted that Rhoda had covered her face with her hands, as though it was she who had received the blow. He sped after Nell, through the door she had left open and down to the beach where he knew she would take refuge.

She was sitting with her back against the sea wall when he found her; her hands buried in shingle, rocking back and forth and muttering, 'She's a witch. She's a witch. She's a witch!' Chanting her fear away between long shuddering sobs.

Ned sat beside his sister, not attempting to console her because he didn't know how, but when she became too exhausted to rock or cry he said, 'We'll tell someone, Nell. We'll go and stay with Tibby until Leah and Mark come back. Tibby will know where they are.'

Nell nodded weakly and accompanied him back to the cliff road.

Tibby welcomed them so lovingly Ned immediately found that life was not so painfully precarious after all. But just as he was about to mention their troubles he became aware that Tibby, for all her attentiveness, was in a worried muddle. There were little piles of books and woollies on the sofa, and shoes half-wrapped in newspaper.

'Are you going anywhere, Aunt Tibby?' he asked anxiously.

'Oh, my pets. It's my sister Millie. She's broken her hip,' she told them woefully. 'I have to go to her. She's got no one else.'

Ned watched his sister's glimmer of hope beginning to disappear, and tried to quell the rising panic inside him. He wanted to beg Tibby to stay but knew that, at that moment, Tibby's life was as painful as their own.

'You'll be all right, my pets,' Tibby said persuasively. 'I've had a chat with that nice auntie of yours and she seems to have everything under control.'

Ned embarked on a reassuring smile but felt it slide away from him until his mouth felt all askew. He didn't trust himself to speak.

Tibby peered into their silent faces. 'Don't fret, my loves,' she said. 'Millie's not done for. I might bring her back here when she's more herself. Do her good, won't it, a bit of sea air?'

'Yes,' Ned croaked, his mouth all dry.

They helped Tibby to pack and tidy her kitchen, eating her biscuits to replace the lunch they might not have, and all the time Ned was thinking: we have to go back, and then what?

As if in answer to his worries, reliable Tibby said, 'I told your Auntie Rhoda I'd drop my key in so you could come and feed old Bill when he's at home,' and she held out to Ned, a bronze door key on a green ribbon. 'Would you do that for me, pet? I know he's an unfaithful old tom but I wouldn't like him to think I didn't care.'

'We'll come in every day,' Ned happily assured her. 'Could we sleep here, perhaps, to keep Bill company?'

'Whatever for, my pets?' Tibby was too distracted to be surprised by Ned's request. 'Old Bill doesn't need baby-sitting. He's on the tiles all night!'

'Well,' said Ned carefully, 'we might have an uncle coming to stay.' He was surprised by his cleverness. 'And there might not be enough room. He could sleep on your couch, couldn't he?'

'If it's all right with your auntie.' Tibby flung her arms wide. 'And if he brings a sleeping-bag. I've no time to be making up beds now.'

'You're brilliant, Tibby,' Ned cried; he would have hugged her if she hadn't suddenly buried herself in a china cupboard.

A taxi called for Tibby and took her to the station. They waved goodbye from her steps, trying to pretend the house next door was not their home.

They walked away from Tibby's front door, expecting to hear Rhoda's call. And when it came they had an answer ready for her. She had, of course, been watching for them from the kitchen window. 'Children, where are you going?' she cried. 'Your lunch is ready.'

Ned turned, slowly, to look at her, but kept walking backwards. 'Aunt Tibby gave us lunch,' he said stiffly. 'And now we're going to meet a friend. We promised.' And he sped away from her hurt look of disbelief.

They spent the afternoon sauntering on a cool beach, while the silence between them filled with words they wanted to say yet couldn't utter, because they were too frightened to let them loose. And as the tide began to roll over the empty sand Ned knew that they were pacing out the hours until Arion returned, because now he was the only person in the world who could comfort them.

Evening appeared in a mountain of cloud above the dark rim of the ocean and Ned began to realize that nothing was certain. Arion's arrival was so extraordinary they might have dreamt it. They might even have imagined the evidence that he'd left in his wake: the tideline of sand and shells; the damp footprints on the stairs.

Nell had the same thoughts. All at once, she burst out, 'What are we going to do if he doesn't come back?'

'Rhoda's not so bad,' Ned comforted. 'She won't let that old witch hurt you again.'

'She can't stop her,' Nell cried. 'She's Rhoda's mother and Rhoda thinks she's sad and ill. She doesn't care about me.'

'She does,' Ned said fiercely. He had to make Nell believe it.

The evening enveloped them in a chill mist. The tide

came in; seabirds called each other home and Nell, who felt she did not have a home, knelt on the wet beach and began to sob.

Ned walked round the hopeless little mound of his sister, begging her to trust him, to trust Rhoda and even Leah who would be home soon. But it was no use, Nell was beyond him. And he began to get angry because he was cold and hungry and wanted to go home. He could manage the witch, he could manage anything if he tried, but he couldn't put heart into the pathetic bundle at his feet. His anger gave way to despair and he sank down beside her and stared at the melancholy grey sea.

A great way off, at the furthest end of the beach, where the water met the rocks in a cloud of spray, Ned sensed a movement that spun his head. Telling himself that hunger was making him dizzy he rubbed his eyes and saw the tiny crowd of distant moving shadows solidify and slide closer into focus, sometimes it seemed to be deep in the water and then skimming the surf like a whirling dust cloud. Although it was a leaden grey day, Ned felt as though the sun was rising.

'You've been watching for me!' Arion looked down as from a great height, and Nell, unwinding herself, stared joyfully out at him.

'Yes,' Ned confessed. 'Nell's afraid to go home.'

'Only you can help.' Nell, transformed, beamed with hope.

They told him their troubles in a great rush, pouring out their unhappiness in a stream of half-remembered events, even going back to the time Leah had begun to leave them for her work. And Ned had the impression that all the angry disappointments that tumbled out of them became absorbed, somehow, in Arion. Kneeling before them he gathered up their troubles as a great

77

sea might receive a torrent.

The children were still murmuring when Arion took their hands and led them off the beach. They chattered happily now, as they walked up the cliff to their home. It wasn't until they stood, all three, facing the front door that Ned began to wonder how Arion would manage to change the situation inside the house.

SEVEN

Gifts from the Sea

Rhoda opened the door without their knocking; she had been watching for them. Her face was red and puffy and wisps of hair had escaped from the neat coil and hung in untidy loops about her face. Ned had wanted her to look her best for Arion.

Rhoda, addressing herself to Arion, said, 'Thank you. Were they … lost?'

Arion looked down at the children. 'No,' he replied, 'they were not lost. I've brought them home because they would not have come without me. They're very troubled. I take it you're the aunt.'

'I'm Rhoda, yes!' She brushed a hand across her face, catching at the strands of hair, smoothing them nervously into place. 'Please come in.'

'This is Arion,' Ned told her proudly.

'I see!' She led them into the living-room where Ned suddenly noticed that Arion's feet were bare and this time, instead of shoes, he carried a large rucksack on his back.

Rhoda hovered uneasily about the room, and then remembered to offer tea, which she brought in on a tray with slices of home-made fruit cake.

Arion watched every movement she made, as though he were measuring her. His scrutiny made her even more self-conscious and she spilled tea into a saucer. She swore softly but with surprising vehemence and said in a harassed way, 'Well, where did you find them, then?'

Arion stroked his beard and said, 'On the beach, of course. They were taking refuge from their grandmother. She badly frightened your niece and I've come to make sure that doesn't happen again.'

He leant towards Rhoda and Ned couldn't see the look that sent his aunt shrinking away from the man and clutching at the arms of her chair.

'She's not well. Didn't they tell you?' she said angrily.

'That's no excuse! No excuse at all!' He more than matched her anger. 'I want you to promise me it won't happen again!'

'Who are you?' Rhoda said defensively. 'You've no authority here.'

Arion stood up. 'It doesn't matter who I am. You've no more knowledge of these children than I have. What matters is that you control your mother.'

'How dare you!' Rhoda, still buried in the chair, blazed out at him, but she looked afraid and Arion, immediately contrite, said: 'I'm sorry, I shouldn't have said that, but I have taken these children's troubles to heart and I think you should do the same.'

Rhoda, pressing her hands against her cheeks, all at once began to tell him of the storm that had driven her mother to the mainland, and how she, Rhoda, had taken two weeks' compassionate leave to be with them all, although she'd received Leah's letter too late to let her know.

Ned, listening to this story, knew that Rhoda was leaving out a whole chapter of events in her catalogue of woe, and that this omitted chapter was perhaps the door to that shadowy room where his memory began. He wanted her to tell them of the time before he and Nell had tumbled into the sea, and of the journey that had led them to this moment with Arion. But he knew that he would have to wait.

Arion listened, somewhat inattentively. He, too, wanted something more, it seemed. He murmured sympathetically, stood up and reached for his rucksack.

But Nell, clinging to the bag, cried, 'You're not going. You can't. You're staying here. He's staying, isn't he, Rhoda?'

'Well...yes!' she agreed. In the face of Nell's desperation she could not have done otherwise.

'He can stay in the turret, can't he?' Nell persisted. 'And we'll give him some supper first and take up a candle and more cushions. He's been shipwrecked, you see!'

Their aunt searched for a response. 'Is it Mr Arion or ...or what?' she ended lamely.

Arion considered this question, as though he had a book full of names to consult before choosing the right one. 'Nonpareil,' he said at last, and with a slight inclination of his head.

'Without equal. How unusual,' Rhoda said arching one eyebrow, not daring, though, to deny him this unlikely name.

'He can stay, can't he?' Nell urged. 'You can't make him go. And can he have supper with us?'

Rhoda backed away from these requests, carrying the tea-tray and murmuring, 'I'll bring some blankets.'

'We'll do it,' Nell cried.

Their aunt left a room sparkling with conspiratorial looks and silent giggles, but Arion put a finger to his lips and shook his head in mock disapproval. And because they didn't want to spoil their good fortune, they controlled their faces as they led Arion up to the turret, and Ned called out, 'We'll show Arion to his room.'

They were halfway up the stairs when Ned saw the grey-clad figure above them. Nell's fingers clutched at his sweater and he hesitated, looking into Grandmother McQueen's stony glare. With a great effort he said, 'Hullo, Grandmother. We've brought a friend to stay.'

She did not move or utter a word and Ned remained frozen to the stair. He heard footsteps behind him and Arion brushed past, mounting the steps in easy strides until he was beside the old woman who shrank into the balustrade as he remarked, 'What fine grandchildren you have, Mrs McQueen. My name is Arion!' and he held out a firm right hand.

Ned saw alarm on his grandmother's face. She eased her hands behind her back and wordlessly watched their progress to the top of the house. The children did not dare to look back at her but were aware of her indignant half-blind eyes, marking them out.

Once in the turret though, with the trap-door firmly closed they gave way to relieved excited chatter.

'She's like a witch, isn't she?' Nell said.

But Arion, who was strangely preoccupied, replied, 'Perhaps. But what is a witch?'

The sky was dark now. Only a pale glimmer pierced the curtain of night clouds and in the room they began to lose sight of each other's features. Then Arion rummaging in his bag brought out a handful of fluted shells and set them in the window. Into each shell he placed a small candle, only a few centimetres high, but thick and rounded like a drum. And when he had lit all these candles the windowed room glowed with magic light.

The children watched Arion's deft movements and fell silent. They felt as though they were part of some special ceremony where they would soon be expected to remember a sequence of mystical words.

'I have something for each of you,' Arion

announced, and brought from his rucksack a strand of glistening shells. He placed these in Nell's open hands, and then brought out something larger for Ned, wrapped in a sheet of aged newspaper.

Nell gazed at the necklace, spellbound by the vast array of special polished shells strung on gossamer fine gold; every one of a different species, except for the pearls, although these varied greatly in size and colour; treasures gleaned from the deepest oceans in the world.

'They were made for you,' Arion told them and his strange opalescent eyes fixed on them a gaze of such intense complexity, they felt that this gesture of giving was more important to him, than the gift itself.

Nell slipped the necklace over her head and stroked the silky shells that hung just above her heart. 'Thank you,' she said softly.

Ned, unwrapping the newspaper, found a mirror and was perplexed. It did not seem quite the right sort of gift for a boy; it was very old and very beautiful. The back and the handle were encrusted with a multitude of tiny shells and coloured pebbles; the mirror itself made, not of glass, but of a substance that radiated a special shiny light.

'A boy does not often look at his reflection,' Arion told him, leaning close. 'Perhaps he should.'

'How could this have been made for me?' Ned murmured. 'It's so old.' And he could almost feel a gentle wisdom spilling into his hands as he touched the shells. 'Is it a charm?' he asked, staring into the milky surface and half expecting a mermaid to peep out at him.

Arion folded his arms. 'They *seem* to belong to you, don't you feel it? Only you can find out if they are charms?'

'This makes me feel safe,' Nell said, curling her

fingers into the necklace, 'so it must be mine!'

'You see!' Arion gave a light-hearted laugh. 'And now, if I'm to share a family meal I'd better make myself presentable.' He opened the trap-door to let them out, and Ned wondered what he kept in the rucksack that would turn him into an everyday family man.

Ned, too, took extra care with his appearance. He combed his hair, changed his sweater, and gave his hands an extra scrub. It was comforting to know that Arion was above him, an accepted guest now and not someone to be anxiously hidden.

Before he went downstairs he picked up Arion's mirror again. Now things seemed to move beneath the glimmer; there was a strange green light behind his mirrored face, as though he was not sitting in his room but squinting up through water. He quickly shut the mirror in a cupboard, not ready to recognize the Ned who seemed to belong to a region of fishes.

They found that Rhoda had laid the table with a white cloth and added wine glasses to the corners of two place-settings. She had borrowed the candelabra from the living-room and set it in the centre. Everyone had two knives, two forks and two spoons; a three-course meal. Had Rhoda planned it, Ned wondered, to make up for their unhappy morning, or had the sudden arrival of a handsome stranger inspired her? And if so, why this change of heart towards Arion? He hoped that Grandmother McQueen would not decide to creep out and spoil it all.

Nell wore her necklace for the occasion and Arion appeared in a shirt of such whiteness Rhoda had to ask, 'How d'you manage on a boat?'

'As well as you do in a house,' he declared, watching her misjudge her pouring, once again, and spill wine on to the tablecloth. 'In fact much better.'

And Rhoda, at last, gave in to the shy half-smile that made her beautiful. Pleased with his achievement Arion let loose a peal of wonderful laughter that rocked through the uneasy house, defeating all the unhappiness, and for an hour, Grandmother McQueen did not exist. It became a feast they would never forget.

Arion told them of his travels, and of the creatures he lived with. He spoke of them with love as anyone else might speak of their children or dearest friends. He told them of a time a dolphin had saved his life, carrying him, wounded, for a hundred miles. And he made his listeners understand the magnificence of whales, their compassion, intelligence and truthfulness.

'And birds?' Nell asked. 'Do you know those, too?'

'Of course,' he said. 'How could I live without the birds?'

She smiled at him gratefully, but all at once, and almost accidentally Arion began to discuss pain, then looking round the table he brought himself to an unsteady halt, saying, 'No! I won't tell you about that tonight.'

'We've seen some of it,' Ned told him, 'on television. We've seen fishermen killing dolphins for nothing, and seals dying and birds in oil.'

'We've all seen it,' Arion said soberly. 'But we haven't felt it. We don't really know what it is like to die slowly because our lungs are filled with poison or our feathers unable to protect us from the killing cold; we haven't been blinded, trapped and paralysed by oil. We don't know the panic of watching our friends die all around us and knowing there is nothing, nothing we can do to save ourselves!' Although his anger wasn't meant for them he couldn't help a

85

sudden furious accusing stare, and in the candlelight his irises turned glistening black. Like the sea his moods changed swiftly: glittering, serene then stormy.

'No,' Ned admitted. 'We don't know about that.'

Arion reached out and touched the back of Ned's head. 'We won't speak about it any more tonight,' he said. '*You're* not a villain, Ned. I'm sorry.'

For an instant Ned thought, hopefully, perhaps this man is really Dorian's ghost. But then why doesn't Rhoda recognise him? 'Will you take us sailing one day?' he asked.

'Why not tomorrow?' Arion said. 'My boat is in the harbour now, with her new mast. I'll take you out all day with your aunt's permission.' He looked across at Rhoda who seemed torn by indecision.

'Please,' the children simultaneously exclaimed.

'I suppose,' she began. 'What about life jackets?'

'I've several, just the right size. I'm always prepared for passengers,' Arion said.

'We-ell!'

'Please?' they beseeched her.

'Just for a while, perhaps ... I feel responsible,' poor Rhoda stammered.

The children gave a joyful cheer while Arion promised gravely, 'I'll take great care of them, you know that, don't you?'

'I suppose so, son of Neptune,' Rhoda said, and this time she sounded certain and unafraid.

'Neptune?' Ned inquired.

'Poseidon, then,' said Rhoda. 'They're one and the same.' She was smiling broadly.' In Greek mythology, Arion was a wild horse, son of the sea god, if my memory serves me right. His right feet were human, his left were hooves, or was it the other way about? And there was another Arion whose voice was so beautiful that dolphins would come to listen to him and, on one occasion, saved his life.' She looked at Arion for confirmation of her story.

'You have me absolutely,' he laughed. 'Though, as you see, I don't have hooves.' And he walked round the table to display his tanned and splendid feet.

'No, indeed,' said Rhoda, glancing at his naked feet with a little start of surprise.

Nell, who had been longing for Rhoda to notice her necklace said, 'D'you like it, Rhoda? It's beautiful, isn't it? Arion gave it to me.'

'Very beautiful,' Rhoda agreed. 'I've seen one like it before, smaller and not as fine, of course.' And she gave a puzzled frown, as though trying to remember something.

After the meal Arion shooed the children to bed while he stayed to help their aunt in the kitchen. Ned must have fallen asleep before Rhoda and Arion came upstairs for he never heard them. When he woke up he had been dreaming his dream of the sea again. This time he had travelled further back than ever before. He was in the back of a car that raced through a moonlit night, shaking and swerving. He wasn't strapped safely to the seat as he knew he should have been, but wedged in tightly beside a sort of cradle. From inside the cradle his baby sister cried and cried. 'Be a good boy, Ned, and hold your sister's hand, I can't concentrate,' the man said. Ned could see the dark outline of Dorian's head in a glow from the headlights. Ned leant over and pulled the baby on to his lap but just as she stopped crying the car jerked to a halt, the man swore and then tipped over into nowhere. Over and over, and Ned had clung to the baby, falling with her to the bottom of the car where he managed to stay until there was a terrible shuddering crash and, in the utter silence that followed, Ned knew the man couldn't tell him what to do, because he would never be able to talk to him again. Somehow Ned had opened a window and climbed out, finding himself on top of the overturned car. He reached inside and managed to wrap his hand round the screaming baby's long skirt, and tugged and tugged until she was through the window…He was standing there holding the baby and not knowing which way to step when he felt himself slipping. He saw the spangled sky, he saw the black rocks below and the stairs tumbling into the sea. He tried to hold the baby but she slid out of his arms and the forlorn white shape plummeted, like a wounded bird, into the dark; in terror and despair Ned had followed her. But at the moment when he thought it was all finished and he would hurt so badly that there would be no more Ned, the shining sea took him and held him and rocked him to sleep.

So when Ned awoke from the dream and saw the oscillating pattern of moonlit water above him, he thought, for a moment, that he was still inside the dream. But the fingers he used to touch the head of his peacefully rocking bed were real wide-awake fingers, and the eyes that blinked up at his glittering ceiling were good clear-sighted eyes that were quite capable of making sense of what they saw. Something had been added to the sensations of the night before; this time he could hear the waves whispering outside his door; splashing in a tumbling, rhythmic cascade down the stairs. The door slammed with a whoosh that was followed by a faint patter, like the spray that blew off the sea and tapped at their windows.

And then there was a scream again. This time more filled with rage than fear. Ned pulled the bedcovers over his head, fighting the voice with all his senses. But the words reached him through all his resistance.

'Rhoda, it's here again. It wants the children. Let it

88

take them, not my Ultramarine, not her. N-o-o-o-o!'
Her rage receded in a low moan and Rhoda's words
fell gently over her mother's grief.

'It's all gone, Mother. It was a dream.'

'N-o-o-o-o!'

Their words became a distant murmur; a door
closed and the house was silent, but only for a
moment. A soft footstep beside Ned brought him
peeping fearfully from the bedclothes.

'It's me,' came a whisper. His sister's voice made
him gasp with relief.

'Are you all right?' he asked. 'Were you listening?'

'Yes,' she said, full of hushed excitement. 'I was
wearing this. It keeps me safe, I think. Look!'

Ned, peering in the dark, found his sister by the
glow that hung, like an inverted rainbow, from her
neck.

'It's the shells,' she whispered. 'I've been wearing
them all night. I didn't feel frightened when she
screamed and said those awful things. I know I'm
safe.'

Ned touched the shells. They gave his hand a
tingling sensation, a tiny magical fizz of pleasure.
'Wow!' he said. 'It's a real treasure. Keep it safe!'

'Of course!' Nell's warm breath fluttered over him.
'Good night!' The glow drifted away, like a friendly
wraith, and the door closed.

Ned thought of his sea-mirror. It held a different
sort of magic. There was no safety in that mysterious
reflection of a boy who lived at sea. There was only an
exciting, and slightly alarming, possibility.

EIGHT
A Dolphin Day

'He's gone again!' Nell woke Ned with a gentle shake. She was fully dressed in jeans and a navy sweater that showed off her new necklace like an heirloom mounted on dark velvet.

Ned dragged himself to a sitting position and looked at his watch. 'Good grief, it's only seven o'clock. I could have had another hour's sleep,' he yawned.

'We're going sailing, remember,' she said.

'Not before breakfast!'

'Oh, I suppose not.' She was disappointed. 'I thought we could go before seeing anyone else.'

'That wouldn't be fair to Rhoda,' he pointed out. 'She'd worry.'

Nell wandered over to the window. 'She knows we're going. It's going to be wonderful. The best day we've ever had in our whole lives.'

'Probably,' he agreed. 'It's funny but, just for a moment, I thought you were called Rainbow. Perhaps I was remembering the words Arion wrote in the sand, or the shells – they had so many colours in the dark.'

Twisting her fingers in the glistening string she said mystically, 'They're magic. They've turned me into someone else.' She drifted out of the room, her head bent over her treasure, and called out, 'Don't be long. I don't want to miss one minute of today. Oh, by the way, the ocean has left his footprints again.'

Ned dressed hurriedly and went to see for himself. Nell was right. There, descending the stair carpet in neat procession, were the same footprints but this time they had a greater depth, as if the bare feet had stepped through the fabric into a pool of still dark water. Ned followed the prints, noticing again the little drifts of sand and shells in the carpet fold at the bottom of each stair, and he became aware that someone was treading softly behind him. He began to hurry, nearly tripping himself up and only looking round when he had reached the safety of the hall.

Grandmother McQueen, squinting at him from the stairs, said, 'Well, you're still here then!'

'Of course I'm here.' Ned felt afraid of her but angry at the same time. 'It's my home.'

'So it is. Mine now, I suppose,' she muttered.

'For a while, yes,' Ned admitted. 'But my mother's coming back soon, and my stepfather.'

'Your mother,' she said peering at him. 'No, she won't come back.'

'Of course she will,' Ned yelled in a panic. 'She's on her honeymoon. She'll be right here with us in just two weeks, you'll see.' Avoiding her hostile eyes he found himself looking at her feet which were surprisingly clad in sturdy leather boots, one of them planted in the centre of a dark footprint. He gave a little exclamation of surprise, partly because he half-expected her to sink up to her knee in an underground sea.

She must have caught the direction of his gaze, and craning her neck sideways, dimly seen her foot set in the dark print. She swung her boot out with a shriek and screamed, 'You wicked boy. You've brought it, haven't you? You've brought it here to swallow me up, well, it's you who'll drown more like!'

He turned away from her and fled into the kitchen, slamming the door behind him but aware that she was following, and unable to ignore the dreadful, quavering voice. 'You'll drown, just like your mother did.'

'No,' Ned cried, his back against the door. 'No!'

Rhoda and Nell stared up at him from the breakfast table, but he couldn't speak directly to them because he was too choked with horror at the thought that Grandmother McQueen had somehow reached Leah with sorcery and in his mind, he saw a Leah-like fish, drowning in the sink, while an old woman plunged a shiny blade into the water.

'It's not Leah that's drowned, is it, Rhoda?' he begged. 'She's got it all wrong. It's Dorian, our dad. Tell her, Rhoda! Make her see!'

Rhoda said, 'Of course, Ned. Leah's quite safe!'

He felt the door handle move in his back and sprang away from it as Grandmother McQueen came in. Rhoda immediately stood up and drew her mother to the table, saying, 'What a surprise. How are you this morning, then, Mother?'

'As well as can be expected,' she muttered, 'with all *that* going on last night. I need my sleep.'

'All what?' challenged Nell, safe within the enchanted necklace.

'You know very well, dear!' Grandmother McQueen did not look at Nell and the unexpected endearment added an extra chill to her voice. '*He* was here!'

Rhoda glanced at the children. She was becoming flustered. 'We had a visitor to stay last night,' she said. 'You know we did, Mother. You met him, but the noise you heard was in your dreams.'

Grandmother McQueen silently considered this. At length she said in a softly malicious tone, 'He was here. Don't try to deny it. Why didn't he take them?' Her voice hissed and disappeared so that they could not be quite sure of her last words.

92

'D'you know who she's talking about?' Ned asked Rhoda wildly. He feared that if he shared the same memory with his grandmother he must be linked to her by something stronger than blood.

Rhoda sighed and, brushing an imaginary wisp of hair from her forehead, began, 'I think we'd better tell you ...'

But all at once, Grandmother McQueen must have caught the sudden sparkle of Nell's necklace. She reached across the table and snatched at the shells, crying, 'That's hers. It belongs to my Ultramarine.'

'No,' Nell screamed. 'It's mine – mine. It was made for me. It's my charm to keep me safe.'

'Safe? That won't keep you safe, dear. It drowned my girl, and it'll drown you, too.'

'No!' Nell leapt away from the table, but her grandmother had coiled her fingers in the glistening strand. The necklace snapped and a shower of pearls and tiny shells rattled on to the table and the floor.

Ned ran to his sister's side and began to gather up her treasures but she couldn't move. Shaking with helpless sobs she murmured, 'No! No! No! She's broken the charm.'

'Oh dear! Oh dear!' chided Grandmother McQueen, busily buttering toast, while Rhoda exclaimed, 'Mother. How could you?' and tried to take Nell in her arms.

'No! No! Go away!' sobbed Nell, shrinking from Rhoda's desperate attempt at love.

Ned gently laid the shells he had retrieved in a little pile on the tablecloth. 'I think there's something you ought to tell us, Rhoda,' he said gravely.

Rhoda, looking at Nell, replied, 'I don't know if this is the right time, Ned. What I have to tell you is very sad and may come as a shock. Perhaps we have had enough sadness for one day.'

'You must tell us,' Ned said fiercely. 'We can't go on not understanding.' He didn't know what he expected to hear. Perhaps that his grandmother was mad, though Rhoda could scarcely say such a thing in front of her. But it had to be told now. A mystery would only creep after them and spoil their wonderful day. 'Please,' he begged.

'Don't mind me,' said their grandmother. 'I'll not stop to hear it though. It's nothing to do with me.'

'It has everything to do with you,' Rhoda said with surprising savagery.

Her mother poured herself a cup of tea. 'Let them know,' she said. 'It won't bring her back,' and as she left the room her face assumed an expression of such desolation Ned found himself thinking he should feel sorry for her. But she had been too cruel to Nell to earn his sympathy.

Nell had returned to the table. With her back to Rhoda she was beginning to thread her shells on to the gossamer strand of gold. Her eyes still sparkled with unspent tears.

Ned eased himself into a chair and waited hungrily for Rhoda to tell the story that might solve at last the mystery of his tumble into the sea.

'Perhaps I should begin with Ultramarine,' Rhoda said uncertainly. 'Or, I don't know, further back, when my father was lost in the sea. He was a fisherman, like most of the Islanders. One day his boat capsized in a storm. He shouldn't have gone out but he was a fearless man and there were four children to feed.' Her voice began to hark back to the lilting accent she must have used before she became that very clever girl who left her island home to further her education.

The children didn't interrupt but waited for Ultramarine's appearance on the scene.

'She was the youngest – I the oldest,' Rhoda told

them. 'Then there was Dorian and next, Zebedee. Grand names for an Island family, but then your grandmother was very different from the person she has become. A great reader she was; she would order books from the mainland library and every week a big package would come over on the boat addressed to Mrs Alistair McQueen. There would be Tolstoy and Chekov and Dickens, of course. Encyclopaedias, Greek and Latin mythology. There would be French writers, Proust and Sartre, translated, naturally, for, to her shame, she only had one language. She would read for half the night, sitting close to the lamp while our father was at sea. She was insatiable. Her eyes became swollen and ringed like an owl. And now she is half-blind and can't make sense of print, and she is probably a little crazy because the stories she consumed have closed above her head; she lives inside them now, and has nothing real left to love.'

'She could try with us,' Ned pointed out.

'Yes, and I know she should,' Rhoda replied, 'but …' Here their aunt hesitated frowning and then, suddenly making up her mind, said hurriedly, 'but the circumstances of your birth have made you into everything she is afraid of.'

Ned postponed the question that Rhoda had led him to ask. Nell was watching him anxiously, and it was for her sake he said, 'Tell us about Dorian, please. He's the one we belong to.'

'Oh.' Rhoda stared curiously at him and then, as if remembering where she was, went on. 'Dorian and I went to the big school on the mainland,' Rhoda told him, 'and so did Zebedee. We stayed with relatives during the week and took the boat home at weekends. I'll have to admit we were all clever and did well for ourselves – all of us except Ultramarine.'

'Why was she called Ultramarine?' Nell asked.

'I gave her that name,' Rhoda smiled. 'She was christened Marina but her pale new-born eyes gradually darkened to a vivid blue and having learned all the clever names for colour I called her Ultramarine. They used the word, long ago, to describe the blue stones that came from across the sea. And that was another reason for her name; she was always by the ocean, you see, crooning to it and to the seals that came to breed on the far beaches. Her face was always turned towards the water; she couldn't have gone out into the world like we did; she would have suffocated. The sea sustained her. I'm talking like a book, I know it,' Rhoda laughed at herself, 'but I can't help myself. My sister's life was like a fairytale.'

'What happened to her?' Ned asked. 'Was there a happy ending?'

Rhoda didn't reply to this last question. 'When she finished with learning she went back to live with our mother on the Island,' she said. 'They were happy for a while, I believe. And then the kelpie came!'

'Kelpie?' Ned knew it was a waterhorse whose mane could be mistaken for the flying surf; a demon who haunted lakes and estuaries, sometimes so cleverly disguised as human he could charm young women and lure them to their deaths. 'Kelpies are only in stories,' he said. 'They're not real!'

'Of course they're not,' Rhoda shook her head a little mischievously. 'It was your grandmother's wild imagination. They always met by the water, you see, Ultramarine and her young man. He was a fisherman but from another island. Your grandmother was insanely jealous of him, she loved her youngest child more than anything else in the world, she wanted her all for herself, besides, her eyes were growing weak even then and she was afraid of depending on people outside the family. But Ultramarine married her young fisherman and sailed away with him.'

Believing that to be the end of Ultramarine's story Ned tried to turn Rhoda back on course. 'What about Dorian?' he asked.

'He married Leah and we were born, but we didn't live happily ever after,' Nell said resentfully, 'because something terrible happened to Dorian while I was still a baby.'

'Part of that is true,' Rhoda agreed, 'but not all of it.'

For a moment Ned hoped that she would tell them that Dorian wasn't dead but remembering the white grave stone and Leah's very real sadness he knew that could not be the part that wasn't true. So what was left? 'We're late,' he exclaimed in a panicky voice. 'Arion will be waiting. We'd better go. Will you tell us the rest tonight?'

'Yes, of course,' Rhoda said almost with relief and she began to swish about the kitchen in her long skirt, finding apples and biscuits, a bottle of lemonade and packets of crisps. 'I should have made sandwiches,' she said ruefully, 'but events have a way of disorganizing me.'

'It doesn't matter.' Ned grabbed the bag she held out to him and prodded his sister with his free hand.

He heard Rhoda call out, 'But, Ned, your breakfast...' and shouted, 'Don't need any,' as he and Nell sped down to the harbour.

They spied Arion's boat immediately because it was the most beautiful. Either a new mast had been fitted or invisible mending applied and now it flew a blue pennant emblazoned with a silver dolphin. Arion's delight at their arrival could not be disguised; he swung Nell aboard with a joyful shout. Ned preferred to find his own route and jumped neatly on to the foredeck.

They used the engine to take them speeding away from the harbour. They bounced through dark water, past the Belen Cliffs and out into a brilliant sunlit ocean. And when Ned looked back the town was melting into a cluster of ghostly buildings that now and then winked fiercely at the sun. Arion stopped the engine; he hoisted the mainsail and a great gust of air caught the canvas and spun the boat round. They were swept into a direction that seemed to have no place on a compass, for it was neither forward, nor backward nor in between. In fact Ned had the sensation of whirling into place, as though a magnet had pulled him through time to where he truly belonged. He had no need to convey this feeling to Nell for she, too, had been caught in this astonishing region outside the life they knew and yet where they were most at home. It had happened before when Leah had taken them on pleasure trips but this time was the best.

A sunlit mist was creeping over the ocean now and the horizon vanished, leaving them in a world where there was no clear division between the sea and the sky; everything was the same shimmering colour of turquoise overlaid with gold, and the only sound the creak of the boom and the gentle slap of water on wood. Arion, at the tiller, had taken on the appearance of someone not quite real; his hair lighter and his eyes sharp aquamarine. He smiled at Ned as he began to play out the anchor-chain and said, 'We'll rest here for a while, until we get a breeze again.'

Nell had fallen asleep and Ned felt himself slipping, inexorably, into the same state. He tried to keep awake because he was afraid that his heart might stop beating, the stillness inside him was so complete. But the warm mist and the gentle undulation of the boat were insistent. He gradually gave in to them and drifted into a deep sleep.

He woke very slowly; there was a voice somewhere in the distance that was extraordinary in its richness; the words were foreign or not words at all for the song was composed of unfamiliar sounds and almost impossible tunes; at last he came to the conclusion that the sea itself was singing. He turned about seeking the source of the music and Nell, who had woken up at the same time said, 'Someone is singing.'

Arion was standing on the foredeck, his body moving in rhythm with the boat.

He looked at the children and commanded, 'Watch the water!'

'Are we awake?' Ned asked, almost pinching himself for some positive proof of this.

'Of course,' Arion said. 'And only just in time.'

For a moment they sensed a tremendous movement under the sea; the surface rippled silver-white and, all at once, a crowd of silvery heads popped out of the water. The boat was surrounded by gentle, smiling, funny faces.

Ned blinked in disbelief and Nell asked, 'Are they real?'

Arion made a high clicking sound and the dolphins closed in. They came right up to the boat and grinned at them, wriggling and inviting. The furthest began to leap out of the water; one flew, shining, clear across the deck.

'Don't make any sudden movements,' Arion warned, 'but lean over very slowly and put out your hands. Don't touch their heads, but stroke their skin, along the side, and on their bellies if you can reach.'

They did as Arion advised and with the first touch on the dolphin's smooth body Ned experienced an unusual sort of recognition. His hand almost shook with surprise but he kept himself steady and the smiling creature turned under his fingers, delighting in the contact, and returning his gaze with friendly affection. Ned knew his instinct was right. They knew each other very well.

'It's so beautiful,' Nell murmured, her outstretched fingers skimming the surface of the dolphin's skin.

'I seem to know them,' Ned remarked. 'But the only dolphins I've ever seen have been in books or on television.'

'All life goes back to the sea,' Arion replied. 'Perhaps you are recognizing yourself.'

Ned puzzled over this remark as the dolphin slipped away from his hand. It sped through the water to a distance of ten metres or so where it began to perform a series of slow acrobatic leaps.

'He's doing it for us,' Nell cried. 'He's showing off.'

But Ned thought it was sheer joy that compelled the dolphin to act in this way; he felt like doing the same thing.

'Go down to the galley and you'll find a bucket of fish,' Arion told him. 'Bring it on deck and we'll give our friends some breakfast.'

'The galley?' Ned inquired. He wasn't sure if he could face another bucket of fish.

'My kitchen,' Arion told him. 'I'll have to teach you a few sailing terms if you're to join me again.'

To repeat the adventure was all Ned could have wished for. He went down into the cabin, not too keen to find the fish but eager to explore the place where he might even sleep one day. He was surprised by what he saw for he had imagined the comfortable cushioned seats he had seen in films. But here there was only a rough wooden bunk piled with boxes and newspaper. The largest of the boxes were empty but others contained bottles and yet more boxes of plasters, tiny

100

splints and even hypodermic needles.

In the galley Ned found the bucket of fish beside a small tin sink. As he carried the bucket on deck he found himself saying, 'It seems wrong. I don't like doing this. It reminds me of Grandmother McQueen.'

'I wouldn't normally feed them, Ned,' Arion said. 'They're quite capable of fishing for themselves. But just for once, I wanted to prolong their stay. I wanted you to thank the dolphins, in the way they can understand.'

'Oh, yes, of course!' Ned exclaimed. He took a fish from the bucket and tossed it out to his dolphin who gracefully leapt to catch it.

But Nell held her fish in her hand and let her chosen creature nuzzle it away from her.

They continued to feed their dolphins in this way until every one had taken a fish and only two dolphins were left; the first two whom Ned and Nell had instinctively chosen. These two swam about the boat, seemingly reluctant to leave them but in the end it was they who had to make the first move.

A light north-westerly had sprung up, almost, as though created by the departing dolphins, for the trail of dark fins led directly into the wind. Soon little banks of spray had completely hidden them; the wind caught in the sail and the boat veered to the south.

'Hold tight,' Arion cried as the children scrambled for safety.

Clinging to the rail they watched the dolphins spin away from the moving boat and then begin to follow. They sped after them, sometimes leaping clear of the water in curves of dazzling silver, but the wind gathered strength and hurled the boat away from them. At length they abandoned their game and their two heads bobbed in the snowy wake, their faces still displaying the happy smile.

101

'They can't lose their smiles,' Ned remarked. 'Even if their hearts were breaking they couldn't show it.'

'But we would know,' Nell told him.

The wind dispersed the mist and drew a canopy of high feathery cloud behind it. The sun retreated and the new deeper light revealed a tall dark island to the south.

'It's Gardeye,' Ned exclaimed. 'I know by the tower. It was a monastery once but now only the birds go there. We call it Guillemot Island.'

'Could we go closer,' Nell asked, 'to see if there are any birds there?'

'There won't be,' Arion told her. 'Guillemots don't breed for another week or so, and, as you know, they live at sea.'

But as they approached the island they saw that many birds had already come ashore. But they were not perched on cliffs and ledges where they usually nested, they were standing in forlorn little groups on the beach. And even before the reason for this became obvious, the children knew that something terrifying and unnatural had occurred.

NINE

On Gardeye

'Oil!' Arion muttered, and his low voice betrayed a terrible anger.

They looked at him, seeing a man they didn't know. His stance became an expression of rage; he seemed stronger, larger and infinitely more powerful.

'Is there a beach on the other side of the island?' asked this grim stranger.

Panic rose in Ned. He couldn't remember what was so essential for Arion to know. He had only been to Gardeye once. A friendly fisherman had taken them on his boat in late summer when the birds had left to live in the winter ocean.

'No,' he began uncertainly. 'Well, maybe. I think there are little bits of beach all round.'

Nell was shaking her head. 'No,' she said firmly, 'on the other side from here there are cliffs as high as our houses, and a few rocks sticking out of the water. The beaches are only on this side and the part facing Hart's Bluff.'

'Can you climb those cliffs?' Arion asked.

'Oh yes,' she replied. 'They are not like a house in that way. There are bits of grass and plants and little tracks that sheep or goats could have made. Leah said the monks probably kept goats for their milk.'

Ned was astonished by his sister's recollections of that long-ago visit. It was all coming back to him now, but only because Nell had fed his memory with such a vivid description.

'We'll get out the dinghy and go that way,' Arion said. 'I want you both to go down to the cabin now and get the rucksacks. There are two small ones for you, and the largest you can find for me. I'll take the boat round to the south-west. We must frighten the birds as little as possible; panic can exhaust and kill them.'

They obeyed his instructions precisely. He took the boat in as far as he could before dropping the anchor. Then, inflating the folded dinghy he flung it into the water and shouldered his rucksack. Still without speaking he indicated to the children to climb into the dinghy. They obeyed and took the oars he handed to them.

'Do you know what to do?' Arion asked, climbing in beside Ned.

Until that moment Ned would not have known how to answer, but at the smooth touch of the oar he found himself saying, 'I think I do.' He had only to watch Arion's deft movements to make this true.

On reaching the island they pulled the dinghy on to the tiny patch of sand and began to follow the narrow track that had been worn into the rocks. It was perilously close to the edge and several times Nell stumbled on loose pebbles, but Arion bringing up the rear, was always there to catch her.

Ascending the last and steepest part of the track they found themselves, all at once, on smooth grass scattered with tiny blue flowers. The wind screeched through the strange stone arch that reared from a mound of fallen stones; but other than the wind there was no sound on the deserted island.

'We must approach the beach from the side,' Arion told them. 'The birds must not be panicked into the water again; it would eventually kill them. Instinct has led them to the beach. Their oiled plumage can't protect them from the cold sea any more and they would die. In your rucksacks you will find gloves and sacking. The gloves will protect you from angry beaks; the birds will be terrified; they are already suffering from something they cannot understand. Our appearance will mean danger; if they begin to panic and run away, don't pursue them. Throw your sacking over the birds with least oil on them, these will probably be the most exhausted because they will have been fighting to stay at sea longer than the others. They are brave little creatures and don't give in easily.'

As Arion spoke he led them past the grass-strewn rubble of the ancient monastery and on to another track that wound down to the beach. They emerged behind a wall of rocks at the edge of the sea and received their first close view of the victims on the beach. The tragedy took their breath away. Dark little corpses lay strewn across the sand, while other birds stood among their dead like mourners in oily black suits; staring helplessly at the sea and occasionally emitting a desolate little grunt of pain.

'Be brave, Nell,' Arion whispered to Nell, whose eyes were huge with concern.

Controlling his rage with an expression of intense concentration, Arion told them, 'We must try to prevent them from going back to sea. I shall go to the furthest end of the beach. Ned, go to the middle. Nell, you must stay this side, close to the rocks. Walk slowly up the beach towards the cliffs. Throw your sacks only over the birds nearest to you. Don't attempt to chase them; they'll die of exhaustion or shock. Wrap them gently in the sacks and put them in your bags. Avoid their beaks at all cost and only take four or five, your bags will not comfortably hold more.'

'But there are hundreds.' Ned stared at the beach. 'What will happen to the others?'

'I'll ring the R.S.P.C.A. as soon as we get back to the mainland.' Arion seemed used to this sort of thing. 'If the birds aren't too frightened they may be able to save a great many more.'

He moved swiftly between the rocks and across the tideline, beckoning Ned to follow. A little chorus of grunts and moans began. Some of the birds started to sway and tumble, others made a desperate attempt to run. The children caught only those who put up least resistance. The others fell back from their approach; their round black eyes desperate, their heavily oiled wings flapping helplessly; some could not be prevented from a wild dash back to sea. But their job was soon over and Arion led them through the screen of rocks with the wrapped birds, grunting against the restrictive sacking.

Ned cast one look back at the scene. He felt helpless, angry and guilty. 'If only we could save them all,' he murmured.

'If only,' Arion echoed gravely.

They didn't exchange another word until they had carried their precious bundles safely back to the boat. They took the birds down into the cabin where Nell and Ned remained gently holding their bags like over-anxious nurses, keeping their patients as still as possible against the swaying of the boat.

They could not say their day had been spoiled because the best of it had been at the beginning. And they had, hopefully, saved a few of the birds. But each knew the other was thinking, Who did this and why? and also that it was one of those accidents that no one cared enough to prevent.

It was only when they began to hear the familiar sounds of the harbour approach, and saw, through the porthole, the reflected lights trickling across the water, that Ned relaxed. His head had been bent over the birds but now he turned it, easing his neck, and saw the letter 'A' scratched into the wooden partition beside him. Putting his finger into the untidy toppling letter he felt his way round the shape and, closing his eyes, found that it was familiar. But he hardly had time to dwell on this strange sensation before there was a command from above to come on deck.

They made a strange procession, the three of them behind their bags, clasping them as though they contained fragile porcelain. When they reached their front door Ned felt for the door key in his pocket and found that he had changed his jeans and left it behind. He pressed the bell and stepped back.

A few moments later Rhoda opened the door to them and stared, uncomprehending, at the grave faces and bulging rucksacks.

'We've brought you some patients,' Arion explained. 'Birds; there's been an oil-spill somewhere. We've rescued a few, but there are more to save.'

'Birds?' Rhoda said uncertainly. 'I don't know...'

'We can take them to the cellar,' Ned said. 'It's dark in there and quite warm.'

'We need boxes, as many as you can find,' Arion called as Ned and Nell brushed past the bewildered Rhoda and made for the cellar door. 'I'll have to alert the R.S.P.C.A.,' he told Rhoda. 'We must work fast. I can probably manage a few more before it gets dark.'

'The phone's in there.' Rhoda indicated the living-room.

From the store of Leah's disused boxes, the children found four with adequate space for three or four birds to move in. Into these they laid sheets of newspaper. 'Never use straw,' Arion told them, as he lowered his birds gently on to the paper. 'Hay and straw often contain a fungus that can harm the birds' respiratory system.'

'There seems to be so much – against them,' Ned remarked.

'Yes!' Arion surveyed the room. It seemed to satisfy him. There was warmth from the large boiler and a sink beneath the only window, which was small and let in the minimum amount of light. A jumble of boxes and garden tools were propped against the far wall with Ned's outgrown bicycle. Otherwise the place was empty. The birds would not be disturbed.

'I must make that phone call,' Arion said, springing up the cellar steps, his bare feet making no sound on the hard stone.

Nell and Ned stared down into the boxes. One of the birds had white rings round his eyes, like a little painted warrior. He turned his head, one eye gazing curiously out at them. Looking into the dark, unblinking eye they couldn't tell if he was afraid of them or angry at being kept helpless in a box.

'He will be all right, won't he?' Nell whispered fiercely.

'He doesn't look too bad,' Ned replied with as much cheerful optimism as he could manage.

Arion reappeared, having made his phone call. 'I want you to look after the birds,' he said. 'They'll need water and fresh fish, sprats or whitebait would be best. Give them clean newspaper to stand on, and keep them as quiet and calm as possible. They can only begin to recover if they feel safe.'

'Can we clean them?' Nell asked.

'On no account! It's a long and difficult process, Nell,' he told her. 'It needs great skill. Tomorrow I'll hire a van and take them to the R.S.P.C.A. treatment centre. Your job is to look after the birds until that time, and if they survive it will probably be due to your care.'

'I'll come with you.' Ned followed Arion up into the hall.

'No, Ned.' Arion turned to him. 'I want you to buy some fresh fish. Offer it to the birds in a shallow bowl, with a little water. I must go, there are so many more to save.' He walked out into the street.

Ned leapt after him. 'But couldn't I come, after I've bought the fish? Couldn't I come to Gardeye again, to rescue the others?'

'No! It'll be getting dark and the wind is already strong. It's dangerous work.' He paced down the hill making no allowances for Ned's smaller stride, and the boy had to run to keep up with him.

'Please!' Ned persisted. 'I'm strong and not afraid.'

At the end of the road before he turned to the harbour, Arion stopped and regarded Ned with a strange watchful concern. 'I know what you are, Ned,' he said, 'but I want you to stay with your sister. Here's money for the fish, I'm sorry I forget sometimes when it must be used.' He handed Ned a five-pound note. 'Off you go. If you can't get fresh buy frozen and thaw them before you feed the birds.'

'O.K.' Ned's route to the shops lay in the opposite direction to the harbour, but as they walked away from each other Arion called, 'Thank you, Ned.' And it seemed to imply something more than gratitude.

Ned had wanted to be alone with Arion, navigating the dark sea without Nell, who always had to be anxiously watched. And Arion had known this.

It was not difficult to buy fresh sprats in a town full of fishermen, and Ned was soon running home with a bag full of fish. He was dismayed to find that he still had no key and once again had to ring the bell.

This time he was shaken by the appearance of his grandmother, who opened the door just wide enough to reveal half of her face and one suspicious eye. Ned made to push past her but she resisted, placing her foot against the door.

'Let me in, Grandmother,' he said urgently.

She removed her foot and as he leapt through the door asked querulously, 'What's that?' and gave the bag of fish a poke.

'Fish,' Ned answered briefly but remembering her appetites added, 'for the birds.'

'Birds? What birds?' She paced beside him to the cellar door.

'Guillemots, they're sick,' Ned explained. 'We're looking after them until our friend can get them to a treatment centre.'

Rhoda emerged from the kitchen. 'They'll be gone tomorrow, Mother,' she said.

'I don't like – birds.' Grandmother McQueen almost hissed the last word. 'You know that, Rhoda. Get them out.' She spoke like an aggrieved child. 'I don't care if they're sick.'

'But you don't even have to see them,' Rhoda said patiently. 'They can't hurt you. They're in the cellar.' As she spoke she manoeuvred her mother into the kitchen.

'They're covered in oil,' Ned said angrily. 'They're dying, some of them. It's people like you who are responsible. People who don't care about anything in this world except themselves. And what have those birds done to you, or to anyone for that matter?'

'Done?' The old woman's eyes had a malicious glint now. She welcomed the challenge. 'They killed my girl, they did. They killed my Ultramarine.'

'No!' said Rhoda, firmly restraining her mother's twitching shoulder.

'I'll have my say,' shouted Grandmother McQueen. 'It was those very birds that killed my girl, them and the kelpie.'

'Mother, don't...' Rhoda began.

'How?' asked Ned impatiently. 'They're shy little birds. They live at sea. How could they hurt a grown woman?'

'Ah, she went to save them didn't she?' His grandmother began to launch herself into this story, almost with enjoyment. 'Just like the kelpie told her to. She was out in her little boat on a clear blue day; she was where she loved to be, singing lullabies to the water, I shouldn't wonder. But the kelpie tricked her, you see; he wanted her with him so he sent those sly little birds, dipped in a bit of oil so that she'd feel sad and try to save them and just as she leant out of the boat – he took her hand, oh, very gently, I'm sure, trying to make her believe it was just a wave. But the kelpie held on tight, him and the birds, and they pulled her down and down...'

'Don't be silly,' Ned cried in a panic. 'There's no such thing as a kelpie. Whatever it was that drowned your daughter, it wasn't birds or kelpies. It sounds to me as though she was just careless.'

She seemed not to have heard him and, for a moment, looked almost calm, then, as if remembering where she was she shouted, 'Oh, they were all alive they were. The boat was full of them. But she was gone. They found her little boat drifting, full of wicked birds, and you don't care.' An astonishing range of emotions passed fleetingly over her weathered face. Ned saw malice and disdain, followed by emptiness and un-relieved pain. 'You don't know anything, do you, you misbegotten children?' She mumbled. 'Well, it's time...'

Rhoda must have sensed danger in those words; she put her hand along her mother's arms saying urgently, 'Don't, Mother. Not yet!'

Ned was aware of Nell beside him, plucking at his

sleeve. He felt tempted to withdraw and run from whatever it was his grandmother was trying to reach him with. And yet, he knew they must wait now while their past spilled towards them. 'It's time for what?' he ventured.

Grandmother McQueen smiled and shook her daughter's hand away. 'Time to know who you are.'

'We know who we are.' Nell's frightened voice spoke up.

'Not quite,' came the harsh voice. 'It's time to learn about Ultramarine!'

'Mother, no!' cried Rhoda. 'Not like this.'

'We know about her,' Ned said in a puzzled way. 'We know about her being your beautiful youngest child with ultramarine eyes, and sailing away with a fisherman, and saving birds – and drowning. It's a horrible and sad story for you, but she's gone and the birds aren't. We can save them, just like she did. She'd be happy about that.'

His grandmother had turned away from him. She was waiting, staring at nothing until he finished and then she murmured into the air, 'You don't know who she was.'

'She was your daughter,' Ned exclaimed impatiently.

'She was your mother!'

The words dropped into the room like a spell and froze them. Ned's mind, battered by the pieces of his remembered past, seemed to shrivel with the effort of trying to reject what he knew must be the truth. He couldn't speak.

But Nell, stepping before him, said fervently, 'It's a wicked, wicked lie. Leah is our mother and you're a witch!'

For the first and last time in their lives they heard their grandmother laugh. It was a dreadful sound.

TEN

Nightingales

Rhoda, suddenly coming to life, stood up and said, 'This shouldn't have happened. Leah should have told you... I never expected that she hadn't... We must talk about it.'

'Later,' Ned said roughly and drew his sister away to the cellar door. 'We have to feed the fish.'

'Let me help!' Rhoda followed them.

'We can do it. Leave us alone,' he said. He had to concentrate; to try and pretend his grandmother's last words were still unsaid, so that they could be spoken in a happier time, by someone else, when Leah was there to make the truth more comfortable.

In the cellar they peered into the boxes and saw the dark forms of the stricken birds, still silently fighting to be alive, and Ned wondered if the worst of their pain was in not understanding what had happened to them. He found a shallow bowl under the sink, and poured five centimetres of water into it. Then, opening the bag of sprats, he placed a few into the bowl and lowered it carefully into a box. He was rewarded with a sharp peck and hastily withdrew his arm.

'You're bleeding,' Nell said, alarmed. 'Does it hurt?'

'No,' he replied cheerfully. 'And it shows they've got a bit of strength left.'

'I can't not talk about it any more, Ned,' his sister solemnly confessed. 'I want her to say it's not true about Ultramarine being our mother. It means we're not us, not who we've always been. Can't we make her take it back?'

Ned shook his head. He rubbed his arm. 'We can't make her take it back because it's true,' he said.

'Don't say that!' Nell cried. 'You're making it worse.'

'Well, I can't talk about it,' Ned said roughly. 'Later, when we've taken care of the birds. We need more bowls, more boxes, they're too cramped in these.' He couldn't push an image out of his mind though, the picture of a young fisherman whose face he couldn't see, a kelpie, perhaps, who must have been his father.

For the next hour they were ferociously busy. Under Rhoda's anxious gaze they raided the kitchen cupboards for roasting tins and shallow dishes. They bought more fish and staggered home under giant empty cartons from the D.I.Y suppliers. Meanwhile, Grandmother McQueen hid herself from all the frenzied activity.

When there were two birds to a box and a bowl of sprats for each one, they left their patients in the warm dark to stay alive until Arion could fetch them. And then the children went to bed. They didn't speak to Rhoda, except to say good night, because they were too tired to think or talk about anything, least of all how they had, all in an afternoon, become the children of two people they had never known.

But in the night Ned woke up again and from his window saw a tiny light, far out at sea, and wondered if it was Arion still at work. Gradually, all the wonderful moments of the past day came flooding back to him, very clear and yet unreal; like a vivid dream that has no place in the everyday world. If he hadn't noticed the damp footprints on his way to bed, he might have thought Arion was someone he and Nell had conjured up to fill an empty place in their lives. But he was real and would protect them.

He couldn't go to sleep now. He was hot and thirsty and his mind was rocking with questions. So he crept downstairs, carefully placing his feet into each magical footprint and receiving from them a strange calm. Everything became clear and hopeful and he knew that he could take a good long look at the truth without being afraid of it. And suddenly he found that he wanted desperately to know about Ultramarine; what she looked like, how her voice had sounded, if she smiled a lot and, above all, how his life with her had been. After all they had been together for nearly three years before Nell was born.

He was surprised to find a light on in the kitchen. Rhoda and Nell were sitting at the table with mugs of cocoa, talking.

'She won't tell me everything without you being here,' Nell said as Ned came in. 'But you'll have to now.' She turned to Rhoda. 'You promised.'

'I wish your…Leah was here as well,' Rhoda sighed. 'It doesn't seem right without her.'

Ned drew a chair closer to Rhoda's and sat beside her. 'She meant to tell us,' he said, 'but she said it was our grandmother's story. Well, *she's* not going to tell us, is she? Not in a truthful way. Her way is going to be all mixed up with hate. We don't want to know about ourselves like that.'

'All the same, Leah should be here to put her side of things,' Rhoda said uncomfortably.

'Please tell us.' Nell stretched her hand across to Rhoda's. 'Please!'

And Ned added, 'From the time she married and sailed away.'

It was not an easy task for Rhoda. It was clear that she had practised the story in her head for just such an occasion and still had not perfected it, hoping that

Leah would have found the moment to tell her adopted children.

'I wasn't there, remember,' she began. 'I had already found a place in a very grand library in Edinburgh. I was so pleased with myself, so happy in that vast storehouse of books, I hardly bothered about the contents of the letters from Ultramarine and Dorian. But I kept them and, afterwards, rediscovered her life and yours. There was one from Leah, after Dorian died, a sad letter but one that was almost a happy ending for your story.'

'It hasn't ended,' Nell said. 'It's only halfway through.'

'You're right, of course.' Smiling, Rhoda continued, 'Perhaps I'd better start when your mother sent her first postcard from the Caribbean telling me that you were born, Ned.'

'What was my father's name?' Ned asked, suddenly faced with an image of himself as a baby, in a strange man's arms, for Ultramarine's fisherman could not have been Dorian.

'Nightingale...' Rhoda struggled for a first name. 'Amos? No, Albie Nightingale.'

'So we are really Nightingales,' said Nell with happy surprise. 'We're not McQueens – I'm so glad.'

'We would have been McQueens if she hadn't married,' Ned reminded her. 'So that bit doesn't matter. Go on, Rhoda.'

'There were postcards from every part of the world, after that. If I hadn't been so happy myself, I'd have envied my sister. There were monkeys from Madagascar, butterflies from the Amazon, tigers from Indonesia, arctic foxes from Alaska. They must have sailed round the world twice over. And then it all stopped and the next time I had word of her it was in a long sad letter. She had returned to the Island to have

116

her second child. 'I thought I could be like him, Rhoda,' she said. 'But I never will be. I couldn't make myself strong enough. I don't think I'll hold this new baby unless I stay on dry land, still and calm. But Mother doesn't make it easy, and my husband has gone away. I know he must but I wish I could keep him on land for just a little while. I did so want a home for my children, and a patch of earth where we could grow enough to live on. I thought he would stay for his boy as they have a very special relationship but he just says, "The sea sustains us, Marina, without it there is no life, and I have no choice but to go because there are men out there who are changing it, and creatures who deserve better than to die the way they do. Six million dolphins have been killed, carelessly, caught with tuna fish they put in tins, for people's lunch or supper".'

Ned was not sure if the last sentence was Rhoda's own, or borrowed from Ultramarine's husband. 'Six million,' he breathed in horror.

'I have never given tuna fish to your grandmother,' Rhoda said earnestly, 'nor would I eat it myself.'

'No,' Nell said, 'nor whales, I hope! You know our mother's letter by heart, just like a school poem.'

'I read her letters so many times after she'd gone I can almost hear every word as though she spoke it, because I wanted to understand why she put herself at risk when you were both so very small.'

'She was saving birds.' Nell excused her mother. 'It's difficult to think of people as well.'

'Can you tell us about our time on the Island, until our mother drowned?' Ned asked.

'It wasn't a happy time,' Rhoda warned. 'She sent one more letter a few months after Nell was born. Oh, she loved you, make no mistake, but without her husband and with your grandmother treating you both like little aliens, like kelpie's children, she couldn't fight. She was proud of the way you cared for your sister, Ned. "My little boy is such a thoughtful child," she said. "I always know the baby will be safe with him, and I think his grandmother is fond of him in spite of herself. He fetches water for her and carries the fish-basket; he finds her lost pins and holds things close to her poor eyes. He refuses to let her hate him".'

'I didn't know all that,' Ned murmured.

'Perhaps some of it was best forgotten,' Rhoda said. 'Sometimes your grandmother got in such a rage over her failing sight, and especially when you talked about your father. Ultramarine had to take you out in the boat for hours, away from the bitter talk. I don't know what made her leave you behind on that last day.'

Ned, glancing at his sister's desolate face, explained, 'She left us because it's dangerous work, saving birds.'

'Of course,' Rhoda agreed. 'She left you because she loved you.'

'And what happened after?' Nell asked in a small voice.

'Well, that's when I saw you!' Rhoda happily exclaimed. 'You were three, Ned, and Nell about six months old. Oh, you were so beautiful. If I'd been a married woman I'd have taken you,' she added wistfully, 'but I'd chosen my life and couldn't change it. We met there, at the Island chapel on a stormy day: Dorian, Leah and I: we made no decisions, then, but I could see how it must end: that Dorian and Leah would take you and keep you as their own. He would have made a wonderful father.' Rhoda's face showed such a sad tenderness they knew that Dorian was the one she missed above all. 'He was a better father to you than that other one, because he saved you!'

'Saved us from what?' Ned asked.

The distress that had already begun to creep into Rhoda's face deepened, all at once, into something very painful. 'I can't,' she began, 'explain to you ... without ...'

'Our grandmother,' Nell said. 'He saved us from our grandmother. I knew she was a witch,' and she regarded the ceiling as though it had a chink in it that might reveal a pair of spiteful eyes.

'She wasn't really cruel,' Rhoda insisted. 'She wasn't herself. She was mad with grief, I suppose. We should have known when we left you with her but she seemed sane then, and confident that she could care for you until all the papers were signed and you were legally Dorian's. But I began to feel uneasy; I went back a week later and found you. She... you...'

They waited, unable to help her.

'She'd locked you in a room and forgotten to feed you,' Rhoda said at last, and almost in a whisper.

'Forgotten?' Ned asked suspiciously.

'Of course, forgotten,' Rhoda said, somewhat defiantly. 'She hadn't even fed herself. The neighbours became anxious, they knocked and knocked but there was no reply, so they alerted the police. They arrived just after I did. You had tried to get out, Ned, by thrusting your small hand through the locked window. It was winter and there was no warmth in the house at all. We came just in time.'

Ned regarded the scar that ran along his forearm. He felt as if confined in a box of ice that was slowly squeezing the life out of him.

'You weren't concerned for yourself.' Rhoda's voice seemed to come from a great way off. 'You kept repeating, "Please help my sister; please save her. My daddy says I must look after her until he comes".'

'But he never came,' Nell said in a tragic voice. 'Never, never, never!'

119

'We took you to the hospital on the mainland,' Rhoda went on, deep in her reminiscences now, and barely aware of the children. 'They let me spend the night there and in the morning I telephoned Dorian to come immediately and take you away. But your grandmother got there first; there was a terrible scene. There'd been a change of plan, she said. Zebedee wanted you, and he must have you. He was rich and famous, not a humble civil servant like Dorian.'

'Zebedee?' For the first time Ned thought of that other brother, a man who had dropped, like a strange parachutist, into their story.

'I knew Zebedee too well,' Rhoda said. 'He should never be anyone's father. We were enemies as children and probably still are, though I've never seen him since he left us twenty years ago. But your grandmother would have it that you should be his. She never wanted Dorian to have anything. Theirs was one of those sad relationships where a child had to fight for his life at every step. She thought Dorian was nothing and never cared to see his generous, kind spirit. She only saw Leah once, at Ultramarine's funeral. Zebedee was her favourite son; he was a wilful, bright boy and entirely selfish. I shouldn't say this of my own brother but he was wicked too; we were all a little afraid of him.'

'But Dorian took us, all the same.' Ned began to realize that Rhoda was nearing the time where his memory began and the man who wanted to be his father had ended his life.

'It was all my fault,' Rhoda confessed. 'I was afraid that Zebedee would arrive at any moment, and all our plans for you would be swept aside. He was like that, as imperious as a thunderstorm. So I told Dorian to drive like the wind, those were my words, and I'll never forgive myself for saying them. I had forgotten

120

that winter roads were treacherous with ice, forgotten the thousand mountain corners that would vanish in snow and mist – and I had forgotten Devil's Mouth.'

'Devil's Mouth,' Ned whispered. He walked over to the window. To his tremendous disappointment Rhoda's story hadn't helped at all. It had brought him to the place where all his strange sea-dreams had begun. It told him why he and Nell had tumbled into the starlit sea but it explained nothing of what he most wanted to know. If only she had said, 'Albie Nightingale was there. He saved you.' Instead there had been nothing but the violent sea.

'You must be very confused,' Rhoda said gently. 'And I won't say it's been all for the best. I've always thought that a useless statement to make when someone is in pain. But Leah has done wonderfully well. You're everything your mother would have wished you to be.'

'What about our father?' Nell enquired. 'Did you ever hear of him again?'

'Never, I'm afraid,' her aunt replied. 'Sometimes we got a hint of where he'd been, but he was always moving on; I even began to think there was no such person as Albie Nightingale.'

'And why did you stay out of our lives till now?' Ned asked accusingly.

'I thought it would be best for you to lose your unhappy past and all the McQueens with it. I am rather too good at convincing myself I'm not needed. I kept in touch though,' she reminded him, 'with little presents and Leah wrote to me so often, telling me how wonderful you were. And now I see that's true. I heard, just in time, that your grandmother was coming here. Leah thought I was too busy and didn't realize I'd have left everything to be with you.'

'Thank you,' Ned said woodenly. 'You saved us

from the witch a second time.'

'Please, Ned, don't call her that,' Rhoda said sharply. 'She's still my mother and your grandmother. Try to think of her as someone who could have loved you if things had not been against her.'

Ned stared into the dark void where he knew the wind and ocean were growing wild and strong. The light had gone now, perhaps Arion was on the far side of Gardeye. How would he save all those birds in the dark? Where was the oil-slick? Would the dolphins, too, be caught in it? 'He'll probably take them down the coast by boat,' he said almost to himself. 'Somewhere that's closer to the treatment centre.'

'You must be very tired, both of you. You'd better get some sleep,' Rhoda advised.

Nell took her empty mug to the sink and joined Ned at the window. 'He'll be back for our birds, tomorrow,' she said. 'Shall we take one more look at them?'

'Can we?' Ned asked Rhoda.

'One more look, then straight to bed,' she said.

They turned on the cellar light and walked cautiously down the steps. The dishes were almost empty and the birds, roused from sleep, were peering furtively out of their oily feathers.

'It's going to be all right,' Nell whispered. 'He'll fetch you tomorrow and take you to have your feathers cleaned, and then you'll get better and be free again.' Ned noticed that she paid particular attention to the painted warrior.

There were little grunts from each box, convincing Nell that they were reassured by her news. Ned thought that they were frightened by the light and sudden disturbance.

'We'd better go,' he said. 'They sound scared to me. I don't think they like the light.'

He didn't think that he would be able to close his

eyes again but he was wrong. He slept very deeply and when he crept into Nell's room, long after their usual breakfast-time, he found her still asleep. He woke her with a gentle nudge and said, 'I'm going out for more fish, back soon.'

He was running out of money, though, and had to search for Rhoda to beg for more. Her bicycle was still outside and her handbag on the kitchen table. But she was nowhere to be found. He couldn't bring himself to knock on his grandmother's door and it was so silent in the room beyond he couldn't believe Rhoda would be in there with her mother. He found her, at last, in the cellar, kneeling in a dark corner. The boxes had all gone.

'What's happening?' Ned cried. 'Where are the birds?'

'Ssh!' she said, pointing under the sink. 'Arion's taken them. He came very early this morning. But we missed one. It must have got out of the box – I can't imagine how.'

Ned, peering beneath the sink, looked into a guillemot's fierce black eye; it was their painted warrior. Ned withdrew a hand abruptly as the long beak struck out at him. The bird seemed to have made a remarkable recovery.

'I'll get some more food.' Swallowing his pride Ned added, 'Can you lend me a pound, Rhoda?'

'Of course, Ned. Come upstairs. Will the bird be all right, d'you think?'

He was flattered that she thought him already knowledgeable enough to give advice. 'We should get it into a box, I think,' he said. 'But it seems O.K.'

In the kitchen she gave him ten pounds. 'It's for you, Ned, all of it. Spend it on whatever you need. It's pocket money, long-delayed.'

'No, Rhoda! I don't need it.' He didn't want her to

know that Leah had forgotten pocket money. 'I'll bring you the change.'

'Please!' She looked at him, so very seriously. 'It's what I would have given you on your birthday this year. You're probably getting a little too old for the presents I might have chosen.'

He accepted the money, awkwardly. 'I think I'll get the fish before breakfast,' he said. 'Our bird might be hungry. Thank you for the money, very much.'

When he returned with another pound of sprats he found Nell in the cellar. 'It's so sweet,' she whispered. 'I wish we could keep it.' She was half lying on the floor, her head propped on one hand, staring at the guillemot.

'It's a wild bird,' Ned told her, 'and a pretty fierce one. Watch out for its beak!' He offered his fish, as before, in a shallow bowl of water, and this time the bird didn't wait to eat alone, it gobbled the fish hungrily.

They put fresh newspaper on the floor and watched the bird emerge from its hiding place under the sink. Its dark head turned anxiously.

'It's like a little penguin,' Nell remarked, watching the bird with tremendous concentration. Ned noticed that she had mended her necklace, the rustle of shells seemed to interest the bird.

'If I hung my necklace round him, like a charm, perhaps he would get better,' Nell said.

Ned shook his head. 'I don't think you should try,' he said.

They watched him taking adventurous steps around the cellar. He appeared to be listening for a sound he might recognize, his head twisted comically to one side and then the other. They couldn't help smiling but when Ned laughed out loud the bird stopped abruptly, frozen into an attitude of caution and alarm. They could neither see nor hear it but the quickened heart-beat reached them, somehow, and they knew that it was very frightened.

'We'd better leave it,' Ned advised. 'It's still in shock.'

Their retreat was followed by the guillemot's vigilant black eye.

'I hope Arion won't be long,' Nell said, closing the cellar door. 'I'm afraid for our bird.'

He arrived before sunset. When he strode into the kitchen they leapt up to greet a furious thunder-cloud.

ELEVEN
Death of a Painted Warrior

'What is it?' Ned cried at Arion's forbidding face. 'Are the birds...?'

'Most of them will live!' Even the voice had changed. It was strident and cold. 'But there are many, many more, and not only birds.'

'The dolphins?' Nell asked fearfully.

Arion's anger seemed to fill the room. 'I don't know yet,' he answered her. 'Seals will certainly be affected. Their food is polluted.' His face relaxed a little. 'I'm sorry, Nell, I've frightened you. There's been a tragedy, nothing I can say will change that, but I'm here to help.'

'What happened?' Rhoda asked.

Arion dug his fingers into his mane of uncombed hair, the first sign he had shown that he might be tired after his sleepless and busy night. 'It was in the gales three weeks ago,' he said. 'A tanker was blown off course and ripped by submerged rocks. They haven't managed to contain all the oil, a million gallons of it is spilling its way across the ocean. The guillemots were only the first visible victims. And as if that wasn't enough, I've just sailed through a ton of floating waste!'

'Can we help?' Nell begged. 'Can we come with you?'

'Not to sea, Nell,' Arion told her firmly. 'But you know what to do if you find a stricken bird. And when you have wrapped it up and brought it home, ring the

R.S.P.C.A. I'll write their number on the phone pad.' He seemed to be on the point of leaving again, reluctant to go, yet anxious to be at work.

'You left one behind,' Ned told him desperately. 'You can't go without helping it.' He had to keep Arion for a few moments longer, imagining that if he walked away now, they would never see him again and if that happened there would always be a terrible emptiness where he had been.

'Please help the bird,' Ned said.

Without hearing the words that Ned had left unsaid, Arion answered two questions at once. 'Of course, I'll help you, Ned.'

They took him down to the cellar where the little creature had again retreated to his favourite hiding place beneath the sink.

'I'll have to clean him here,' Arion said, removing his jacket. 'I'll need some sticking plaster and somewhere where there's a shower.'

'Leah's is detachable,' Nell said. 'I can bring it down here!'

'Good. And the plaster. We must keep his beak closed, though he'll probably attempt to use it. Ned, I want you to fetch Rhoda. It needs two of us.'

'Can't I?' Ned asked.

'No!' He was detached and efficient, this other Arion. 'It's too risky. Get your aunt.'

'Arion wants your help,' he told Rhoda, somewhat sullenly.

'Mine?' Rhoda stared out at him as though such a thing was impossible.

'Yes. You're to help him clean the bird. We're not – capable enough, it seems.'

'Clean the bird,' she repeated in a scared and rather foolish way. 'But I can't. I never have. I don't know…'

'Well, he'll tell you,' Ned said resentfully. 'You've got to.'

She looked so awkward and unsure, peering out of her unruly hair, Ned was, all at once, reminded of the comical little bird and had to smile. 'It's all right,' he said. 'I'll show you how.'

He led her down into the cellar where Arion had already captured the bird and taped its beak. 'You must hold it very firmly. Keep its wings down.' Arion addressed Rhoda rather in the manner of a teacher advising a helpless schoolgirl.

Realizing she had no option, Rhoda took the bird saying anxiously, 'I don't want to hurt it.'

'You won't if you hold it correctly,' he said. 'First I shall have to remove every scrap of oil with a cleaning agent, then I must wash off all the cleaner. If this isn't done correctly the plumage will lose its water repellancy. It could take over an hour.'

'An hour,' she complained. 'I'm not sure I can.'

'It's a life,' Arion said fiercely. 'Children, you can leave us now. Rhoda is nervous. We must discuss the operation in detail.'

They left. Both of them quietly angry.

'It isn't fair,' Nell declared, closing the cellar door. 'We could have done it.'

'He knows best,' Ned told his sister. 'Let's do the lunch for a surprise, and then he'll have to stay a bit longer.'

Nell was too agitated to be of much help. She pulled bacon out of the fridge and put it back. She took side plates out of the cupboard and replaced them with the large embossed dinner plates.

'We ought to have something special,' Ned said thoughtfully. 'A sort of farewell meal. It sounds as though he might be gone for a long time.' He couldn't bring himself to say forever.

'He can't go,' Nell cried. 'I don't want him to.' Unable to express her feelings she screwed up her face and began to roam about the kitchen, tapping fitfully at the furniture.

'That won't help.' Ned tried to sound reasonable. 'I'm disappointed too but it's no use being possessive about someone who doesn't belong to us. When Leah and Mark are back things will improve. She's still our mother.'

'It's not the same now, though, is it?' Nell dropped into a chair. 'Not now we know about ourselves.'

'I can't argue with you. I'm going out to find something a bit more exciting than all this everyday stuff.'

He left her, hugging the back of the chair; cross and hurt.

The delicatessen seemed to be the best place for something unusual. Ned bought Italian salami, French cheese, green olives and pitta bread, believing that foreign food would please an adventurer.

As soon as he stepped inside the front door he knew he should not have left the house. He found Nell slumped across the table and when he gently turned her face toward him he found it shining with tears.

'What is it?' he breathed, believing her to have been overwhelmed by all the frightening new knowledge of their past.

'It's our grandmother,' came Nell's choked reply. 'She took the fish that was for the guillemot. I tried to stop her but...but...' Her voice collapsed with distress.

'But what?' Ned urged.

'She took my arm in her fingers that are like claws and said all sort of slow and mean, "Who's brought me a fish then? Where's my dinner?" and I said, "The bird is dying, Grandmother. It must have that fish; you can eat anything." That really made her mad; she screamed at me and hit my face and called me kelpie's child; and I could feel her hating me so much I wanted to … to just disappear, so there wouldn't be a me to hurt or hate any more.'

'Why didn't you call out?' Ned exclaimed. 'Rhoda or Arion would have heard.'

'I couldn't,' she said vehemently. 'They're trying to save our bird. If we stop them now, perhaps the cleaning won't work. And I love the bird so much I want him to be free; flying and swimming and being as happy as a bird can be. If he dies I…' She shook her head miserably, tilting it up to him so that the glittery tears shouldn't spill again.

Ned turned away and flung his bag of food on the table. He felt lost but knew he must present a calm certainty. He must keep Nell safe from her fears. 'Help me to lay the table,' he commanded. 'The bird has enough fish for now and I can always get some later. When Arion comes up I'll tell him about our grandmother.'

'But he's going away,' Nell reminded him. 'What can he do?'

'I don't know,' Ned almost yelled at her. 'We've got to hang on, Nell, just until Leah comes back.'

She stared up at him, her flushed face showing not an ounce of hope. 'I'll try,' she said, in a pathetically resigned way. But as she began to move around the table, shuffling knives and forks into place, she suddenly asked, 'What is a kelpie, anyway? Is it human?'

'It looks human,' Ned told her and then, in an effort to turn his grandmother's accusation into a compliment added, 'It's very handsome, I believe. That's why maidens were attracted to it. But it turns straight away into a sort of sea-creature when it has its human victims in its power, and takes them under the water, where they drown, of course.'

'And Grandmother McQueen thinks our father was a kelpie,' Nell murmured, frowning.

'Only because she's an angry, superstitious old woman,' he said. 'It probably made her feel good to think her daughter was stolen away by something not quite human, as though she couldn't help herself.'

'I wish we had known them,' his sister said sadly. 'Albie and Ultramarine.'

Ned could find nothing comforting to say for he was wrestling with the same problem. He wondered if there was a photograph, somewhere, that he could put beside his bed and maybe talk to before he went to sleep. 'Anyway,' he said almost to himself, 'when you come to think of it, kelpies can't be villains now; because it's us who are killing them, with oil and nets and polythene and a hundred other things.'

'All the stories will be turned inside out,' Nell said without looking up.

An hour later Rhoda and Arion emerged, surprised and delighted to find such an interesting meal prepared for them. Rhoda's cheeks were pink with modest triumph. 'If anyone had told me that I should one day hold a fierce little bird for nearly two hours, I would not have believed them,' she said, cheerfully rubbing her aching fingers.

'Perhaps there are many good things you don't know about yourself,' Arion said gently.

'Will he really be all right?' Nell asked anxiously.

'He's very weak,' Arion said, 'but with rest and quiet he should get better. Tomorrow, if he's strong enough, Rhoda will ring the R.S.P.C.A. and they may be able to get him to the treatment centre. They have ponds there, where birds can test their cleaned plumage. If all goes well he will be released with the others, in a place that's still free of pollution.'

After lunch they accompanied Arion to the harbour,

even Rhoda who now treated Arion like an old friend. Ned tried to keep himself in a positive frame of mind but as the boat dwindled and faded towards the line of gold that rimmed the stone-grey sea, he found it difficult to believe that the flash of white that moved about the boat was not the brilliant crest of a wave, or the flying mane of a wild sea-horse that leapt across the bows. He began to imagine that Arion was vanishing into the sea that had brought him and he could not organize his face to hide the dismay he felt.

'Why so downcast, Ned?' Rhoda inquired, but without waiting for his reply, went on, 'Your friend will be back again.'

'He didn't say when.' Ned looked into her gentle face finding as much confusion there as there was in his own heart.

'It can't be too long, I'm sure,' she said.

Something had happened in their absence. A breath of gloom met them at the door and an unnatural emptiness crept about them as they entered. Intuitively, Ned went to the cellar door. The light was on and his grandmother stood at the foot of the stone steps, clutching at her chest. 'Help me!' she croaked.

Rhoda ran past Ned, crying, 'Mother, what is it?' But Nell, standing close to his shoulder, whispered fearfully, 'The bird!'

They descended the steps, deaf to their grandmother's wheezy muttering. 'My heart, Rhoda. It's my heart. They've done for me,' she whimpered.

'Who, Mother? cried Rhoda in terrified concern. 'Why are you down here? What possessed you?'

The children silently passed the two women, and stepped side by side to the centre of the room where they turned and turned, desperately searching for their helpless patient.

It was Nell who found the bird. She didn't make a sound but dropped to her knees and remained for a moment, utterly motionless, her back straight and arms hanging helplessly at her side.

Ned had to look away and with closed eyes saw again the dove-like baby falling from his grasp and down into the abyss. When he glanced up Nell was getting to her feet. She had folded the bird into her arms and held it close to her face; but the dark head drooped unnaturally, the sharp beak was harmless now and the black eyes veiled with grey.

'He's clean,' Nell said with wonder, 'completely clean. He can fly again and swim without ever feeling cold.'

The irony of her sad little speech unleashed Ned's fury and, instinctively shielding his sister with an outflung hand, he wheeled to face his grandmother and bellowed, 'You killed it! I know you did, you wicked old woman. I hate you, do you hear? You're evil, you are. You're all the terrible wickedness in the world rolled up and spat out in a mean horrible old thing, and I wish you'd get out of our house and leave us alone!'

With one hand clinging to the stair-rail, Grandmother McQueen gradually subsided on to the lowest step, her free hand held out to Rhoda.

'Ned, don't,' Rhoda cried.

'Well, how do you feel?' Ned asked. 'You've just done the most wonderful thing in your life, probably. You've helped to save a bird and now she's killed it.' He pointed at his grandmother as though with deadly accuracy he could inflict a mortal wound.

'You don't know that,' Rhoda objected, but horror and pity collided in her face. In happier circumstances she might even have looked funny.

'Of course, I know,' Ned furiously went on. 'Look at

133

her hands. He pecked her with his last bit of strength. Look! Look at the blood.'

It was true. Rhoda couldn't deny it, but Grandmother McQueen, clasping her daughter's arm, whined, 'I can't see, dear, you know I can't. That thing attacked me. I only wanted a little bit of fish. No one thought of me. I haven't had my dinner.'

'You're disgusting,' Ned said contemptuously.

As Grandmother McQueen continued her fretful whimpering Nell walked quietly past and mounted the steps. With head erect she was oblivious to the anger swirling in the little underground room; she rose out of the clouds of fury, with the bird held close and tight, for all the world as though the little creature was keeping her alive.

'Where are you taking it, Nell?' Ned called, frightened by that vacant, faraway expression.

She didn't reply but pushed the door open and let it slam behind her. Ned felt an urgent need to follow his sister and to prevent her from doing something that might be dangerous, but he hadn't recovered from his outburst and it wasn't until Rhoda spoke to him that he managed to jerk himself into action.

'Go after her, Ned,' she said. 'I must see to your grandmother.'

Grandmother McQueen was slumped against her daughter; her eyes were closed and her face, behind its dark complexion, had a fading, ghostly quality.

Ned rushed after his sister. He knew he was too late as soon as he heard the soft thump of the trap-door above him. But he continued to climb the stairs until he reached the red spiral leading to the turret.

'Nell?' he called, anxiously. 'I think we should bury the bird.'

There was no reply.

'Nell,' he said, trying to sound matter-of-fact. 'I

134

don't think it's a good idea to be up there with the bird.'

No sound came from above, but he knew she was there.

'Please talk to me,' he begged.

The profound silence was broken by a shuffling in the hall. Rhoda had emerged from the cellar. He heard her go into the living-room and make a phone call. It was very brief. A moment later she was mounting the stairs. She came to the landing beneath him and said, tonelessly, 'Ned, your grandmother is seriously ill. I've called an ambulance.'

'Oh!' he replied, too preoccupied with his sister to care what his grandmother's trouble might be.

'They'll be taking her to hospital,' Rhoda went on. 'How is Nell?'

'I don't know,' he said. 'I'm staying here until she talks to me.'

'Yes, that's best.' She spoke like an automaton; no feeling in her voice at all.

All at once he saw the situation from Rhoda's point of view and felt very sorry for her. 'You'll want to go to the hospital with her, won't you?' he asked tentatively. He didn't want to be alone in the house with Nell so distant from him; he didn't know if he could cope.

'I think I'd be of more use here,' Rhoda said, her voice receding as she descended the stairs. 'I won't leave, Ned.'

He felt instantly relieved. He could stay at his post for a while. In a few moments he would knock on the trap-door and try to get a response from Nell. If there was none, Rhoda would be there to help him decide what to do.

Ten minutes later an ambulance drew up outside the house. Rhoda went to the front door. There was a brief discussion and movement in the hall that gradually retreated down into the cellar. There followed silence, and then a concerned conversation as the ambulance-man manoeuvred a stretcher through the cellar door. Ned allowed himself a brief glance down the stairwell and caught a glimpse of his grandmother's disappearing grey head, resting on an equally grey blanket. She wasn't play-acting now, her immobility was too definite to be unreal.

He dropped back to his position under the turret door. Through the sharp sound of the siren he heard Rhoda close the front door and walk into the living-room.

She'll sit by the phone, Ned thought, and wait for her news while I sit here and wait for mine.

When the whine of the ambulance had died away he crept up the spiral and tapped gently on the trap-door. This time he tried a different approach. 'Are you hungry, Nell?' he asked softly. 'Would you like a drink?'

'Bring some fish,' she commanded in a surprisingly steady voice.

'What for, Nell?' he inquired, and received the answer he dreaded.

'For the bird, of course,' she said.

He didn't know what to do and then found himself saying, regretfully, 'It's dead, Nell!'

He should have used some other, better words. He could almost feel the silent intake of breath that greeted his unwelcome statement. Nell was fighting to disbelieve him. Perhaps, if he brought the fish, she would open the trap-door and he could talk to her face to face, give her food and drink. But to bring a fish would be like lying, it would help her to slip so deep into unreality that he might never be able to bring her back.

Ned wandered downstairs to find Rhoda. She was, as he had guessed, sitting close to the telephone.

'I don't know what to do,' he said. 'She thinks the bird is still alive.'

'Leave her for a bit, Ned.' Rhoda motioned him to sit beside her. 'She'll understand eventually, people do.'

'What if she doesn't?' He searched her face for signs of doubt but found only a sad resignation.

'Then I'll phone Leah,' she said wearily. 'Mrs Tibbs gave me a number for emergencies. I didn't want to use it but if Nell really…'

'I don't think Leah will be able to help,' Ned broke in. 'There's only one person Nell will believe. She'd give the bird to Arion. He saved it so it's his in a way. He'd make Nell understand. I wonder why he seems to be part of the ocean sometimes?'

'They say that life itself began in the sea.' Rhoda leant back in her chair, letting her eyes wander to the mysterious grey mass, flecked with seemingly motionless breakers. Far, far out a patch of gold showed that the sun had found its way through the leaden sky. 'Perhaps that's why water soothes us when we watch it,' she went on, 'like a visible lullaby rocking us back to babyhood where we lived safe in someone's arms.'

Ned looked at her, an image dawning of Rhoda in her mother's arms. 'How is Grandmother?' he asked.

'She's had a heart attack,' Rhoda replied, frowning. 'There's nothing to be done until we find out how bad it is. At the moment she's just very frightened.'

Unable to stop himself, he said, 'Like the bird was, before it died.'

'Like the bird,' Rhoda agreed, her voice faint as a whisper.

TWELVE
Arion's Story

Ned couldn't do justice to the meal that Rhoda had cooked so carefully, and nor could she. They listened for footsteps and frequently turned to the door.

'I'll make some cakes,' Rhoda suggested. 'When Nell smells baking she'll get hungry and come down.' She set to work again.

But Nell didn't appear.

'She won't eat when she's unhappy,' Ned told his aunt. 'She won't let herself.'

They tidied the half-eaten supper away and went into the living-room again, where they sat and watched the ocean. Long silky clouds gathered over the horizon: a meeting of great sky-whales whose shadows changed the sea from sparkling silver to deep ultramarine. Rhoda sat with her hands folded in her lap, patient and calm and, although she never spoke to Ned, he drew comfort from her presence and the strength to be patient with his sister.

When the cakes were cool, Ned climbed the stairs again to tempt Nell with her favourite food. But there was no reply. He didn't expect one. He went and fetched the fish because to trick her into opening the door without them seemed unfair, and once deceived she might never believe him.

'I've brought the sprats,' he called. 'You asked for fish, Nell, and I've brought them. I promise.'

The door was lifted a few centimetres and he saw a doubting blue eye. He raised the bowl of sprats so that it could be seen quite plainly. Nell opened the door wider and stretched down her hand.

'I've got cake and orange juice as well, d'you want it?' he asked, as she lifted the bowl away.

She didn't answer so he quickly tucked them over the lip of the opening before she let the door fall again.

'Are you going to sleep in there?' he called through the closed door.

'Yes,' came the reply.

He took this news to Rhoda who shrugged and sighed, 'Well, as long as she's had a drink I suppose she can't come to any harm. I don't see that we can do any more.'

'I think I'll go down to the sea,' he told her.

'Not for too long, Ned,' she said. 'It's getting dark.'

He understood that to have two children lost or out of control would be too much for Rhoda when her mother was drifting into the dangerous region between life and death.

'No, not for long,' he replied, already at the door.

She gave a brave smile and said, 'I'll ring the hospital again while you're out.'

The beach was empty, the sea like glass. The waves came in tiny rolling curves that ended in a gentle splash and only a hint of spray. Ned sat as close to the water as possible. He had it in mind to talk to the ocean. But could find no words to convey his thoughts. He sensed a mysterious intelligence, hovering before him, just out of reach. Perhaps the sea knows what I want better than I do myself, he thought. And if that is true what does it make me? A kelpie's child. Is Grandmother McQueen right after all? Do my dreams of the sea mean that I am not quite human?

This alarming thought burst from him in a little cry that was echoed, uncannily, by a crowd of birds,

139

flickering over the water. They swung away, with a high plaintive clamour: oystercatchers, their scarlet legs bright against the black plumage. Ned, remembering the oil slick, called, 'Don't go too far!'

But then oystercatchers don't hunt and swim like guillemots, Ned recalled; they rely on shellfish gleaned from the beach. He waited for the restless crowd to return and when they failed to appear began to imagine them haunting the sky above a vast and empty sea; lost and comforting each other with song. And in his mind's eye he saw a white-sailed boat skimming towards them, over the glassy water, and the birds, so pleased to see it, circling the sails and calling, 'Help!' And Ned could see a man on deck, looking up while the birds echoed their message. But he couldn't tell if the boat turned then, or sailed on toward the deathly black tide that bled from the dark horizon. Ned shivered. He had promised Rhoda he would not be long. He retreated from the sea and went home.

Rhoda wore a guilty look of pleasure; she was different from the aunt he'd left only half an hour before. 'I've phoned Leah,' she told Ned. 'You don't mind, do you? I think she has a right to know about Nell.'

'You shouldn't have,' Ned blazed. 'I can cope with Nell. After all Leah's not our mother.'

'Ned, how dare you,' Rhoda returned, angrier now than he had ever seen her. 'She's loved you and cared for you for eight years. I know that. And I'm afraid I can't cope with Nell. I shall have to spend more time at the hospital. Your grandmother is deteriorating very fast.' She took a choking intake of breath. 'Leah wants to come home. She'll be here late tomorrow. I had to tell her, Ned, that you know about Ultramarine.'

She walked away from him and a few moments later

he heard a door close above him.

He was alone in a kitchen that sparkled with tidy cleanliness. Rhoda had obviously tried to distract herself with domestic chores and the room looked positively spring-cleaned. The long table was bare except for an open book, lying close to the place where Rhoda had been sitting. And because everything else was neatly stacked or out of sight, Ned felt the book draw him like one living thing might be drawn to another in an otherwise empty world. He sat in his aunt's warmed chair and glancing at the open page saw the name Arion. It gave him an odd thrill to see his friend's unusual name lying before him and an intense curiosity to know why Rhoda should have been seeking him in a book. Had she come upon the name by chance? Ned thought this unlikely.

He looked at the cover and read the title out loud: *Heroes of Greek Mythology*. It was not at all the sort of stuff that Leah left about when she had time to read but then Rhoda was a librarian, her life was all books; she had a thousand titles at her fingertips; she must know a million stories and exactly where to find the hero she wanted.

'Arion of Lesbos, son of Poseidon,' he read and paused to wonder over this before continuing with Arion's story printed in a smaller type beneath the bold heading.

Ned read greedily. He had always been a fast reader but now he devoured sentences so quickly that they began to build a world around him, so real and colourful it seemed to be clearer than the contours of the room where he sat. And in this fantastic region he found Arion of Lesbos, whose music won for him treasures of gold and whose rich voice so delighted dolphins that, in a moment of great danger, they had carried him through the sea to safety. And later the god Apollo had immortalized the dolphin, and set him in the night sky, a cluster of blazing planets.

With mounting excitement Ned began to wonder if their Arion was immortal and had been sailing the oceans for three thousand years or more, watching with dismay and anger the destruction of his world and all the creatures who drew their life from it. When Ned closed the book he felt quite shaken. He realized that he didn't want to believe his friend was a phantom from the past. He didn't want the help of someone unnatural who, by some magical feat, might solve problems in such a fast and temporary way, they might resurface as soon as the spell faded. And there was no magical answer to his need. 'I want to know who we are,' Ned said to the hero within the closed book. 'I want to know that Nell will be safe without me.'

He took the little grey book to his room and, before turning out his light, read on; delving into the stories of gods and heroes whose lives flowed through each other with love and violence. They were not true, all those tales, Ned reasoned and yet, recalling the unseen presence that had lurked beside the sea, he realized that the legends did not have to be true, and the gods did not have to be seen, to make them any the less real.

Outside, the quiet sea moved gently under a sky that was heavy with stars. Ned wondered in which part of the hemisphere the god Apollo had scattered the handful of stars that made Arion's dolphin. He wished he knew more about astronomy. He thought of Nell in her uncurtained turret surrounded by that glittery sky. Before he fell asleep he crept, blinking, into the dark beneath the trap-door. 'Are you awake, Nell?' he called in a hoarse whisper.

There was no answer.

'Good night, then,' he called automatically.

He didn't like to think of her sleeping with a dead bird in her arms but there was nothing he could do about it.

He was awakened by a strong salty smell and went downstairs to find Rhoda grilling bacon.

'I thought it might tempt Nell out,' she said.

'It's tempted me.' Ned, still in pyjamas, sat at the table and gulped down his tea.

Rhoda looked pleased but wary. Ned, translating her expression, waited for bad news.

'I don't know what to do,' she confessed sliding a plate of bacon and eggs towards him. 'I want to go to the hospital but…'

'We'll be all right,' Ned assured her, tucking in.

'It's not that simple, Ned.' She disappeared briefly to fetch the milk from the doorstep. 'I can't leave you with Nell locked away up there!'

Ned sighed. 'I'll go and give her a shout when I've finished my breakfast. She'll come round, I know she will.'

Rhoda poured herself a cup of tea. 'Did you find the book I left for you?' she said, her grey eyes scanning his face over the rim of her cup.

'Yes,' he said, noncommittal.

'I thought you might find it interesting.'

'I did. Rhoda, d'you think Arion took the name Arion for himself because he … he …'

'Has a fine voice and an affinity with dolphins?' she finished for him.

'And being a sort of "son of the sea" he went on. 'You said Poseidon was another name for Neptune. And there's that other Arion, Neptune's son, a wild sea-horse!'

'That's true!' she affirmed.

'I mean he can't...' Ned struggled. 'It isn't possible, is it, that he could be a ghost of one of those Arions, or both?'

'I must tell you, Ned, that I believe in ghosts,' she said, 'but Arion seems too positive to be a mere phantom.'

'Do you think the sea has tricked us into believing that he is real?'

'Do you mean an illusion?'

'I don't know what I mean, Rhoda,' he said desperately. 'He knows so many everyday things and yet there's something incomplete about him. It's as though he had to plant his footprints so deep into the house he would not forget to come back. And when he sleeps here it's as though there's no one really there, but the sea takes his place so that he won't be missed, like a sort of – foster parent. Nell and I both felt it, and so did Grandmother McQueen.' Another idea struck Ned, this one so wonderful and astonishing it made him gasp aloud, but he kept this last thought to himself.

'Ned, what is it?' Rhoda asked.

'Something I suddenly invented,' he told her, then taking the conversation back to its beginning he asked, 'Have *you* seen a ghost? You said that you believed in them.'

'As a matter of fact I have,' she replied. 'When I was a child. At first I thought it was my brother Zebedee playing tricks, but now I'm more inclined to believe that he called it up. Zebedee was like that. He claimed to have seen all sorts of people from the past.'

'Who was it?' Ned leant closer.

She hesitated a moment. 'Our poor father,' she said at last. 'He was lost at sea.' She got up and went to the sink where the morning sun struck her face and Ned couldn't tell if she was shielding her eyes from the

144

strong light or the memory of her father's ghost.

'It was horrible,' she said and Ned couldn't bring himself to ask for a description.

'Didn't our grandmother ever like us, Rhoda?' he asked. 'Not one bit, even when Nell was born?'

'Yes!' Rhoda said, and then more positively, 'Of course! She must have!' She said this as though something had arrived in her mind just in time. 'Of course she did,' she said again. 'She made a night-dress and covered it with real lace. Ultramarine told me in an early letter how your grandmother sat night after night, working so close to the lamp it almost burned her. Your mother warned her she would lose her sight altogether, the stitches were so tiny, but she persisted; she made herself forget the kelpie so that she could make the finest lace for her granddaughter. She must have loved Nell then, don't you think?'

'Very much,' Ned replied. 'Where is the nightdress now?'

'I've no idea. Perhaps your grandmother still has it.'

Ned finished his breakfast in thoughtful silence and went upstairs to get dressed, telling Rhoda he would try to make Nell come out. He couldn't think why he had heard no sound from his sister, and when he went up to knock on the trap-door he discovered why. The door was very slightly open and the turret was empty.

Ned stood scanning the sea, the cliffs and the rocks beneath, knowing it was useless because Nell would be hidden beyond the bluff. He was sure that was where she had gone. He wondered whether he should keep his sister's disappearance a secret and allow Rhoda to visit her mother in peaceful ignorance but he realized that, even if he managed to control his alarm, deceit might cause even more trouble. He walked slowly downstairs trying to compose a sentence that would convey his news without sounding too disturbing. But when he found Rhoda in the living-room, she knew immediately that something was wrong, so he didn't bother to use reassuring phrases. 'She's gone!' he said.

Rhoda's left hand flew to her mouth, her right hand to the phone, but something happened to startle her even more than Ned's alarming news, and she remained frozen in this awkward attitude.

Ned turned to discover the source of her astonishment and couldn't prevent a little jump of surprise. Arion stood in the doorway, his hair dark glistening with drops of water.

Ned, fighting to control an urge to run to Arion's arms, told himself that this man was still a stranger and might even be a ghost. There was something unreal about that silent appearance; it caused a strange disturbance in the air almost as if the house itself gasped at such an unnaturally sudden arrival. But a pleasantly down-to-earth voice explained, 'Your front door was open.' Then, looking from Ned to Rhoda, 'What's happened?'

'My sister's gone,' Ned replied. 'She was acting a bit weird and now she's run away.'

'Why?' Arion demanded.

Ned glanced at Rhoda. 'The guillemot died,' he said, and because the man stared at him in such a commanding way he had to add, 'Our grandmother must have frightened it.'

Arion's expression took on the thundery look they had come to know but Rhoda cried out defiantly, 'She couldn't help herself. It's all over anyway. She's beyond blame; she had her punishment long ago, before all this.' She slumped into the chair that was supporting her, covering her face with her hands.

'Grandmother's very ill,' Ned told Arion. 'She's in hospital and Rhoda wants to be with her. I think I

146

know where my sister's gone.'

The stormy look subsided and Arion began to show a profound sympathy. With a few quiet strides he was beside Rhoda, touching her shoulder and smoothing the wayward wisps of hair in such a gentle and somehow personal way that Ned had to look away.

He became aware that Arion was almost lifting Rhoda from the chair, settling her into her coat, fetching her bag. Then Rhoda was composing her face and clothes with fluttering movements of her long hands while Arion phoned for a taxi. She was looking at Ned now, and forcing a smile from him as Arion said, 'We'll find her, Rhoda. Trust me!'

'I'll have to!' She gave an awkward little laugh and added, 'I'm so sorry. I don't know what came over me. I'm generally a very calm sort of person.'

'Of course you are,' Arion agreed with a penetrating look, 'but you must give others a rough passage occasionally.'

The local taxi arrived promptly and Rhoda departed with grateful backward glances, trying her best to keep at bay the shadowy sadness that kept falling across her face.

'A much undervalued lady,' Arion murmured as the taxi carried Rhoda out of sight. 'Now we must see to Nell. You say you know where she is.'

'I think I do,' Ned told him. 'I'm almost sure she'll be on the beach below the bluff. It's her favourite place because she can see Gardeye from there and watch the birds.'

'Lead the way then, Ned.'

They closed the door on the empty house and struck off up the cliff path, Arion with strides that Ned, who loved walking, found he could match with ease. He was beginning to lose the shuddery feeling that had followed Arion's unexpected return. The man beside him moved solidly against the sky, depressing the soft mountain grass with feet wearing very ordinary black boots. He was more real than anyone Ned had ever known.

'Why did you come back so suddenly?' Ned asked.

He was subjected to such thoughtful scrutiny from the sea-green eyes, he hardly dared to hope for an answer. 'It must have been the birds,' Arion said with a smile. 'They were so insistent.'

'Oystercatchers?' Ned ventured.

'Of course,' Arion replied.

They walked in companionable silence to the bluff. Here it was bleak and unpromising; the sweep of thick colourless grass broken only by grey rocks humped furtively behind the bracken. Even the curlews called uneasily in the grumbling sky, and the wind had a vicious streak in it. The path to the beach seemed even more perilous than usual. The sister Ned knew would never have come here alone.

There was no one on the narrow strip of sand. They paced the beach, calling Nell's name until they were hoarse, silencing the birds with their rough shouts. Ned became frightened. He could think of nowhere else to look. Nell had no other favourite places, no special haunts, no friends. He found himself looking at the wild sea with terror, remembering how Ultramarine had died.

THIRTEEN

An Exultation of Larks

Drawn closer to the ocean Ned began to scrutinize every shift in the shades that patterned a wave. He peered into the great caves behind the falling spray, dreading to see strands of dark hair or a lifeless white arm.

He had almost forgotten that he was not alone when he felt the hand on his shoulder. 'What made her run away?' Arion asked.

'I told you it was the bird,' he said. 'She loved it. She's never had anything else, you see. No cats or dogs, not even a hamster. The bird sort of – filled her thoughts. And she was already in a state before it died.'

'Why, Ned?'

Ned grimaced, biting on the uncomfortable story that Rhoda had told them. 'We learned that we are not who we thought we were.' He glanced up at the man beside him and found in Arion's expression a look of guarded curiosity.

'In what way are you not the children you thought you were?' Arion asked, exploring Ned's face.

'Well, we are not Leah's real children,' he explained. 'And we don't belong to her husband Dorian either; though Dorian was our uncle. We are Nightingales. Nell liked the name at least.'

'Who told you these things?'

'It began with Grandmother McQueen. She threw the truth at us in an ugly way. But then Rhoda sort of rounded it off. She told us how and why so that we understood.'

'You know who your parents were, then?' Arion, standing very rigid, looked out at the waves.

'Our mother was called Ultramarine,' Ned told him, 'because her eyes were very dark blue, and she was always by the ocean. She was drowned when she was saving birds. It's strange, isn't it, that I wrote her name in the sand the first time that we met?'

Arion's smile did not give an answer. 'And your father?' he asked.

'He was a fisherman called Albie Nightingale, who went away when we were very small and never came back. That was a cruel thing to do, wasn't it? He just discarded us like bits of rubbish.'

'Perhaps he was on the other side of the world when he heard that his wife had drowned,' Arion suggested. 'And no one could find him to tell him the truth – until it was too late and you had become someone else's children. He didn't desert you, Ned. No father could desert children like you. If he stayed away it would have been because he thought you stood a better chance to lead a normal, human life without him.'

'I wish we'd known who we were right from the beginning,' Ned said. 'Perhaps Nell wouldn't have been the way she is, so shy and mystical. And it wouldn't have been a shock, finding out in such a horrid way, without Leah being there.'

'I'm sure Leah did what she thought was best for you,' Arion said, almost reprovingly.

'Yes, she does love us,' Ned admitted. 'Even though she had to go to work, we've always been safe and wanted. She's done everything for us. But I've always felt responsible for Nell. Even before the truth came out, I've always known that there were

150

just the two of us in a way I can't explain.'

Arion gently drew Ned round to face the line of cliffs that faded blue into the distance. 'Don't look out to sea, Ned. Let's be optimistic. There are a great many beaches to search. There are rocks and caves and cliff paths to explore. Nell could have wandered for miles, walking off her unhappiness until she'd gone too far to come back.'

They began a long journey south, for it was obvious Nell could not have gone north past the great finger of rock that stabbed deep into the sea, below the Belen Cliffs. It was a rough walk; they stumbled over the barnacled rocks, slipping sometimes into pools that overflowed their boots, trudging the corrugated sand, and all the time calling Nell's name into the cliffs that sent their voices back to them, mocking and hollow. They had no strength for conversation but Ned kept turning over in his mind Arion's suggestion that Albie Nightingale had not deserted them. And the incredible and wonderful idea that had edged into his mind the previous evening began to grow more solid and more possible making him shout at the impervious cliffs with renewed vigour.

They came to the last bay, where a great wall of rock, far too steep to climb, made further progress impossible. Even a goat could not have navigated its hostile black height. Ned turned desperately away from it, still shouting, his voice near to breaking – when he saw a pale face, barely discernible against the dry sand. He raced over the beach, his voice now failing him altogether.

Arion reached her first. She didn't respond to their urgent voices.

She lay tucked into a shallow depression between sand and rock, her eyes closed, one hand flung out in a gesture of exhaustion.

151

'Nell?' Arion said, bending close, and this time, to Ned's overwhelming relief she moved, frowning as she brought her cold arm closer to her face.

'Nell?' Arion spoke again, keeping his voice low and gentle.

She opened her eyes and stared up at him. 'Hullo!' she said.

Ned, dropping to his knees, cried, 'Nell, you shouldn't have. You shouldn't, we thought...'

'I'm sorry.' She sat up. 'I had to get the bird back to the sea. He was unhappy in our house. I went further than I meant to – I don't know why.' She looked at Arion and said, 'You came back. Did you know about us?'

'I do now,' he said, helping her to her feet. 'Can you walk, Nell, or do you want a ride?'

'I'm all right,' she said, her stiff walk rather belying this.

He allowed her a shaky progress across the beach but when they had slipped round the rocks and out on to a long sweep of sand, Arion handed Ned his rucksack and hoisted Nell on to his back. Handicapped in this way, he raced Ned to the second rocky barrier. As Ned streaked ahead of them Arion shouted, 'You're an athlete, Ned. I've never been beaten on land before!'

'You can hardly run in the sea,' Ned said. 'Unless you mean a sailing race.'

'Swimming, boy!' Arion exclaimed. 'I mean swimming.'

'Who has beaten you at swimming then?' Nell craned down from his back.

'Every dolphin I have ever known,' he declared and his hearty laugh scared a crowd of gulls from their gory feast beside the waves.

'It would be quicker to walk home across the top.'

152

Ned had observed a grassy path scored against the cliffs that mounted the rock in long leisurely bends. It would be easy to climb.

'A great idea!' Arion released Nell, who ran happily to the beginning of the track.

She led the way, leaping ahead with such carefree steps Ned could not help the suspicion that she was hiding something even from herself. It was as if she was burying an unpleasant truth.

When they stood at the top at last, on a high plain of grass and flowers, the sun came out, warming their hands and faces almost as a reward for their efforts. But Ned, still not content, had to ask, 'What did you do with the bird, Nell, the painted warrior?'

'I let it go.' Her smile was curiously cunning. 'I just opened my arms like this,' she demonstrated, flinging her arms in a wide arc, 'and it flew away.'

'That can't be true.' He couldn't help himself. He felt he had to bring her down to earth. 'The bird was dead.'

'No, he wasn't,' she said quickly. 'He was just tired.'

Arion was looking from one to the other with an anxious frown.

Ned didn't know what to do. She was inventing a silly lie for them and it mattered because Arion deserved the truth. She still wore her shell necklace and taking a gamble he said, 'You can't tell lies inside a charm of shells.'

She looked at him, defiantly, then slowly slipped the necklace over her head. 'I'm not lying,' she said, 'but I don't want to test the magic. It wouldn't be right.'

'We mustn't have these gloomy conversations on a day that is going to be so splendid.' Arion drew them away from the cliff-edge. 'Come on now. I've got a feast in my bag and need somewhere to enjoy it.'

'How come you're carrying a feast around?' Ned asked.

'I'm never without,' Arion told him.

They set off towards a tumble of old stones that promised shelter from the wind, but halfway towards it a mass of larks flew out, almost at their feet, spiralling into the sky with gloriously tuneful calls.

Arion held the children still, following the larks with his strange vivid eyes. 'D'you know what that is?' he asked.

'*They* are larks!' Ned made a subtle correction.

'*That* is an exultation,' Arion told him. 'A crowd of larks is called an exultation. Isn't it a perfect name?'

They watched the little birds, still singing, still rising, and agreed that 'flock' would hardly be an appropriate word to describe creatures that bounced on invisible passages of air, almost lifted by their own song.

If only we could throw off all our problems, Ned thought, we might fly like that and even sing.

They found a sunny spot beside the bleached stone ruin. The wind moaned through deserted rooms behind but couldn't reach them. And Arion kept his word; he produced a feast of cheese and crusty bread, melons, dates and even a pineapple, which he sliced with a wicked-looking knife; its carved handle was inlaid with mother-of-pearl. 'A trophy from my travels,' Arion told them, and Ned, running his finger along the satiny patterns, seemed to know his way among them.

After they had eaten, sunshine and soft thick grass dragged them all into a contented sleep and when they woke up the sun had moved deep into the south-west.

'It's late,' Arion observed. 'I hope no one is looking for us.'

Ned thought of Rhoda who might, at that moment,

154

be sitting at her mother's bedside, too deep in her own trouble to think of them. But Leah might have reached home.

For a few moments longer, they sat enjoying the feeling of being adrift from the world with only the birds for company. Then Arion stood up, and as he moved blocking out the sun, Ned asked, 'Who *are* you, Arion?'

The tall man frowned down at him and for a moment Ned thought that he was about to learn something that would change his life but, after a strange hesitation, Arion replied, 'I don't really know.' And Ned had thought his friend knew everything.

'Well, I know who you are,' Nell declared. 'You are Arion. Can't *you* remember your past?'

'I remember my past very well,' he said. 'But if you want to know my lineage I'm afraid I'll have to disappoint you.'

'That's a very grand word, lineage,' Ned complained. 'I just want to know where you came from and if you've got a wife somewhere.' Perhaps he had hoped for too much.

'I don't have a wife,' Arion said sharply, and then, relenting, he knelt beside them and explained. 'I can't even prove where I came from. Someone found me, a baby beside the sea. I was naked but for a few words carved in wooden beads around my neck. My name, I suppose. I was fostered by kind people who had no children of their own. They taught me to read but I never learned to swim, I seemed to have been born knowing it. When I was thirteen my foster parents died and I began to earn my living on the sea.'

'Couldn't you even guess who your true parents were?' Ned asked.

'Yes, I did try and put clues together as children do when they are trying to solve a mystery.' He looked at Ned and continued, 'There was a girl living alone near the sea; a beachcomber who used to watch me swimming. I learned that she had been disowned by her family for having a child out of wedlock. I liked to imagine that I was that child.'

'Why?' said Nell, astonished. 'I wouldn't like to think that my mother was a homeless sort of person.'

'She was beautiful,' Arion said. 'She was kind and she had a wonderful way with creatures. There were always birds nesting near her little stone shelter. She had the face of an angel, she was like...' Arion regarded the strands of cloud that had begun to drift across the sun. 'Yes, I still like to believe she was my mother,' he said.

'But she abandoned you,' Ned protested.

'She could barely feed herself,' Arion said. 'She must have thought I stood a better chance of survival with other people.'

'And what about your father?' Ned asked. 'Did you wonder about him?'

'Oh, no!' Arion laughed. 'I never had any doubts about him. He couldn't have been anything but a kelpie.'

The children stared at him, wanting it to be a joke, yet knowing he was completely serious.

'Are you explaining your footprints?' Ned challenged. 'Our stairs were stained so deep I thought I could see the ocean in them, and there were shells and sand where you had walked. Are you telling us that you are not quite like other human beings?'

'Listen,' Arion said gently. 'I am seldom on dry land. The sea is my home and I am happy there. It is an infinitely surprising and secret place. Perhaps some of its mystery still clings to me when I come ashore.' He stood up abruptly, the confiding mood quite gone. 'Come on now, we've got a long walk ahead of us,' he said.

Unable to question him any more the children had to run to catch up with him and he wouldn't let them stop, even to take an extra breath, until they reached the last few metres of the cliff path, and by then they were too tired to talk.

When they turned on to the road the first thing Ned saw was Leah's red car outside the house. He stopped walking. Everything had changed. He wasn't sure how he would greet Leah. Would his new knowledge become a void between them so that they could never reach each other in the old way? He stood anxiously gazing at his home.

'What is it, Ned?' Arion asked.

'Our moth...Leah is back,' Nell told him, pointing at the car.

'I see,' he said. 'I hope she hasn't been at home too long. She'll be worried.' His own pace quickened, leading them urgently towards the house.

Passing beneath the living-room window they saw Leah's worried face turn towards them; she gave a joyful smile and then she was opening the door and gathering her children to her exclaiming, 'My darlings, where were you? Rhoda warned me I might not find you at home, but I couldn't help worrying.' She led them across the hall, an arm round each neck, and pressed so tightly to her that they almost stumbled together into the room where Mark was standing, a great smile of welcome on his tanned face. He didn't force an embrace on them but patted both their heads murmuring, 'It's wonderful to see you. I'm sorry you've had a rough time with your granny, but everything is going to be all right now!'

Leah drew the children down on to the sofa. 'We'll never leave you again,' she said looking gravely into Nell's eyes, and then at Ned. 'I promise, children, I promise.'

You don't have to say that, Ned thought. We know you will want to go away again, you have to, but next time there'll be Tibby, or maybe even Rhoda. We understand.

After a moment of awkward silence, Leah withdrew her arms from them and clasped her hands in her lap. 'I'm sorry you had to find out about everything the way you did,' she said. 'But it won't change anything, will it? You're still mine – and Mark's.'

Ned became aware that, on the other side of Leah, Nell was isolating herself in a tight corner of the sofa. 'This is our friend,' she said as Arion walked in. 'He came looking for me.'

His quiet entrance caused a breathless sort of surprise in the room. Leah and Mark were speechless for a moment. Ned believed that Leah had read something extraordinary in Arion's face. Arion held out his hand and Leah said, 'Thank you Mr...?'

'Arion,' he said, holding her hand almost a second too long. He went over to Mark, who was not so astonished as Leah but could only manage a brief, 'Mark Howells. I'm glad to meet you – Arion.'

'Rhoda rang from the hospital,' Leah said. 'She told me what happened this morning, Nell. I'm so sorry about the bird, darling.'

'It got better,' Nell said flatly. 'It flew away.'

'Did it?' Leah looked doubtful. 'But how wonderful.' She turned to Arion. 'Please, Arion, sit down. I'll make some tea.' She left them to talk while she retreated to put the kettle on and sort out her thoughts.

Arion asked Mark for a description of his holiday.

158

Obviously at a loss as to what sort of conversation to have with this unusual person, Mark was only too happy to recount the highlights of his brief honeymoon.

Ned left them and went to help Leah in the kitchen. Nell was keeping to her corner, her legs curled under her, watching Arion's face intently.

Ned stood awkwardly inside the kitchen door. 'I'm sorry we spoilt things for you again,' he said.

'We had a wonderful four days. It was all I needed, darling.' Leah was just the same. Her gold-brown face was not altered in any way by his knowing about Ultramarine.

His relief came in a sigh that he was hardly aware of. 'I'm so glad you're back, M...' Only the name stuck. 'I think I'll call you Leah, now,' he said.

Leah, wonderfully encouraged, hugged him again and said, 'Ned, I meant it when I said I wouldn't leave you. Although one day you'll probably find you can do without us oldies.' She laughed and then said, almost shyly, 'As a matter of fact I might be at home all day soon, Mark and I rather want to have a baby. What d'you think?'

He was surprised but found that he was very pleased. The baby would not be the same as he and Nell were, of course, but then... 'We could teach it everything we know,' he said happily. 'Nell would love that. It would be a brilliant baby!'

'Ned, you're wonderful,' she cried. 'And now it's present time,' and rummaging in her bag she brought out two huge golden eggs, one wrapped in turquoise ribbons, the other in scarlet and silver. She held out the egg with the turquoise ribbons. 'It's the kind you like,' she told him. 'Plain chocolate with toffee inside.'

'Thank you!' Ned took the gift. It was so unexpectedly gaudy it astonished him. 'It's lovely!'

'It's an Easter egg, Ned,' Leah said with a laugh. 'Had you forgotten?'

'Yes,' he admitted. 'I don't know why. I suppose there's been so much else happening.'

There were so many things that mattered more than Easter eggs. The strangers who had come to their house had led him and his sister away from the ordinary world; he doubted they would ever find their way back. The path that carried other people securely through everyday events was now lost to them. For Leah's sake he would always pretend to enjoy the things that other children did, and it wouldn't be difficult because Leah was good and kind – she was their best friend.

Leaving his Easter present on the table, he picked up the tray of tea things and carried it into the living-room. Leah walked behind him, carrying the egg with silver and scarlet ribbons.

Ned placed the tea-tray on the low table in the centre of the room. As he bent over the cups to arrange them on their saucers he heard Leah say,' Your present, Nell. The prettiest Easter egg I could find.'

And Ned knew in the moment's hesitation before Nell spoke that she was going to punish Leah for leaving her with a dangerous grandmother and a terrible discovery.

'I don't want it,' she said slowly. 'There's nothing real about it, and even if there was I shouldn't want it.'

She snatched the egg from a dismayed Leah and hurled it across the room. It landed with a dull crack against the table.

In the appalled silence Ned knelt and picked up the misshapen lump of gold. 'You don't mean that, Nell,' he said.

FOURTEEN
Albatross and Rainbow

Nell didn't reply. She pulled herself out of the sofa and ran from the room, vanishing just as the telephone shrilled; another shock that sent Ned reeling back, still holding the rejected lump of gold.

But Leah, welcoming the distraction, seized the receiver and pressed it, almost lovingly to her face saying, 'Leah Howells, here!'

Very little was said at the other end of the line for Leah followed her first words almost immediately with, 'Oh, Rhoda. I'm so sorry,' then, 'Yes, of course!' There was a click on the line before she replaced the receiver and told them, 'Grandmother McQueen has died!'

Mark cleared his throat and said, 'Oh, but that's terrible,' adding ambiguously, 'the poor woman.'

Without referring to the tragedy, Arion stood up and said, 'You'll want to be alone.'

'No, there's no need to go,' Leah told him. 'I'm afraid we didn't know her at all, you see. But I feel so sorry for poor Rhoda.'

People usually cry when grandmothers die, Ned thought. But here they were, only showing dutiful signs of regret. His own last message to her had been the cruellest he could achieve and now she had slipped through his hands before he had truly known her. He closed his eyes because the tired desolate old face came peeping into the room and tried to make him look at her. 'I'm sorry, Grandmother,' he whispered.

161

'What is it, Ned?' He felt Leah's hand on his arm. 'Sit down, darling. It's all too much, isn't it?'

Ned allowed himself to be drawn close to Leah on the sofa. 'It's not that, exactly,' he explained. 'It's just that she didn't even like us and now I'll never be able to make her see.'

'See what?' Mark sat on his other side.

'That we're all right, Nell and me. That we wouldn't have hurt her even if we – if we are the children of someone strange.'

'Whatever do you mean, Ned?' Leah said. 'What has Rhoda told you? You're perfectly ordinary children, with perfectly ordinary parents.'

'Oh, I don't think so,' Ned told her gravely.

Arion, who had been standing, almost motionless by the door, began to move through it saying, 'I've a great deal to do. I must go.'

'What have you got to do?' Ned leapt up. 'Where are you going next?'

'You know very well,' Arion told him sharply. 'They're dying out there.' He seemed to be accusing everyone. Even Leah and Mark stared at him in guilty surprise. 'So I can't waste time,' he went on, 'when I'm needed elsewhere.'

Ned could have said, '*We* need you,' but Arion had never spoken to him so savagely. Ned stood stunned and heard the front door slam. Only half the mystery had been solved. The family were alone at last, but not together. They were each in a little cell peeping out at one another, hoping to be recognized. But was that possible when he and Nell were still not quite whole?

At least Leah and Mark knew each other, all the better for being away from them, it seemed, for Leah was in Mark's arms, tearfully complaining, 'She blames me, I suppose, for keeping the truth from her. I thought it was the right thing to do.'

'You couldn't have done better,' Mark soothed. 'Nell will understand. Be patient.'

'What about you, Ned?' Leah asked. 'D'you wish you had always known about Marina?'

'Ultramarine,' Ned corrected. 'Yes, I do. It wouldn't have changed the way we were. But I'm sorry now that when I was very small I didn't talk to her ghost or think about her on that lonely beach with Albie Nightingale. I could have loved you both, you know.'

'Oh!' Leah brushed her cheeks. 'D'you think Nell feels that way?'

'I don't know,' Ned replied, 'I'm never sure about Nell.' And again he felt the baby slipping out of his arms. Suddenly inspired, he asked, 'Can we see our birth certificates? You've never shown them to us. But I suppose there was no need.'

'Leah had good reason, Ned,' Mark said defensively.

'I know. I'm not accusing her,' Ned assured him. 'Only we've got nothing else, no photographs or letters. I could show it to Nell. It might help if she could see our parents' names, perhaps she wouldn't feel so – lost.'

Leah left Mark's side and went to her desk. 'Your names are different,' she said nervously.

'Really?' Ned exclaimed. He felt devious. He had guessed their names would be different.

'They were unusual. I thought you'd be more comfortable with ordinary names, names that were short and easy to write.' She unlocked a drawer and drew out a long brown envelope. 'If you really think it will help,' she said, still reluctant.

'Yes, I do!' Ned took the envelope but he couldn't open it in front of them.

As he turned to leave them Leah asked, 'The bird, Ned, did it really fly away? I thought from what Rhoda said that it was quite dead.'

'It was,' Ned replied. 'But Nell can't seem to tell anyone the truth.'

'I don't know what Nell would do without you, Ned,' Mark said. 'We couldn't have gone away, you know, if we hadn't trusted you so completely. You've been great!'

'Well, we're the same, aren't we?' Ned remarked with such a small sigh they never guessed how he longed not to be responsible Ned any more.

He took the envelope up to his room but he was afraid to draw out the paper that would tell him who he really was. Perhaps I want to be Ned always, he thought. If I know my name, now, I can never go back. I shall be the other boy forever.

He stood by the window and became aware of a strange rumbling activity on the horizon. The cleaning operation was drawing closer to them. Two planes suddenly rattled over the house and headed out to sea. Soon they would be pouring dispersant on to the oily water. It might keep their beach clean but it wouldn't help the creatures already struggling for life.

He drew out a slim folded sheet of paper. It was disappointingly small for such an important document; his parents' gift of a name. There was only one word at the top of the paper. Ned stared at it, enlightened and astonished for it was not a name at all, it was a bird. 'Albatross,' he murmured, remembering Arion's footprints marking out the word so clearly in the sand; he repeated his description, word for word. 'The most truly marine of all seabirds, they live on the wind and sleep in the sky. They could circle the globe without stopping if they wanted to, and they only follow man by choice, owing him nothing. They are truly free!? Free!' Ned repeated softly.

He was almost sure he knew Nell's name now. He pulled out the second birth certificate and found, at the top, the name he had expected, and yet he felt shaken by the discovery. It wasn't proof, of course, and Arion might never be persuaded to tell. Would it please Nell to know she had been given the name Rainbow? Would it make her feel safe enough to tell the truth about her bird?

Ned sat back on his bed, the two scraps of paper on his lap. He didn't know what to do next.

A car approached and stopped outside the house. He heard Rhoda's voice and the car drove away. Ned thought of Grandmother McQueen, sitting by her lamp, stepping through the strange stories in her books. He hoped the last story she had lived in had been a happy one. Carefully pushing the papers into their envelope he opened his door and ran down the stairs just as Rhoda walked into the hall.

'Hullo, Rhoda,' he said. 'I'm very sorry about...it wasn't my fault, was it?'

Rhoda looked up at him and said, 'Of course not, Ned. She shouldn't have wandered into that dark cellar. Is everything all right here? I forgot to ask for news.' She looked pale and, somehow, very alone.

'We found Nell,' he said and began to walk down to her, but Leah came into the hall so he stopped and watched them. The last time Leah and Rhoda had met had been when Dorian had died. He wondered how they would greet each other. But Leah and Rhoda didn't use words. They fell into each other's arms. Ned decided to go upstairs again.

Later they all had a meal together. It was a very quiet affair. Rhoda, Mark and Leah had already discussed the sad details of Grandmother McQueen and there seemed nothing left to say. They had probably talked about Nell, too, Ned thought. For they glanced meaningfully at each other when she appeared. Ned had a foreboding that Nell had merely come down to punish Leah by not eating. He was right. She sat, pushing her food round her plate with a determinedly woeful expression on her face.

At last Ned spoke up, 'What will you do now, Rhoda?' he asked.

'Go back to work, of course,' she said in a surprised tone.

'But you've taken two weeks' holiday. Why don't you enjoy the last one?' Ned reasoned.

'Ned, in the circumstances,' Leah intervened.

'I'm sorry,' Ned apologized. 'I know it wouldn't be easy for you to enjoy yourself, exactly, but you're so good with birds. You could help – out there.' He nodded at the sea, deep blue in the window.

Rhoda stiffened. 'I only did that once,' she said. 'It doesn't mean...'

'They need all the help they can get.' Nell, coming to life, earnestly took up the cause.

'Nell,' Leah exclaimed. 'Poor Rhoda has a lot to do. When someone dies you can't just go off and enjoy yourself.'

'They can see to things for you.' Nell gave Leah and Mark a challenging look. 'After all you stayed with us while they enjoyed themselves.'

'That is true!' Mark said quietly. 'We could make the arrangements for you, Rhoda.'

'Arion would take you,' Nell persisted. 'He hasn't gone yet.'

This news seemed to disturb Rhoda even more, but she didn't reject their plan. 'I'll think about it,' she said gravely.

She would go if I could join us all together in the way that I know we are, Ned thought. But how could he prove those names in the sand were not a coincidence?

166

When a complicated discussion of funeral arrangements broke out, the children decided to leave the table. Ned silently followed Nell to the top of the house where he told her, 'Leah has given me something for you!'

'I don't want it,' she said.

Ned grabbed her arm and dragged her into his room. 'What's the matter with you?' he hissed. 'You can't keep on hurting Leah. It's not her fault that she isn't your mother. She's a whole lot better than some real mothers are.'

Nell's reasons were quite unexpected. 'I know, but I want her to be my real mother,' she blurted out. 'I always did. I want to be like her. I want to be pretty and kind and clever like she is, and now I know I never will be!'

'Don't be ridiculous.' Ned shook her away. She landed on the bed and immediately buried her face in the pillow. 'She's going to be right beside you for as long as you want her to be,' Ned went on, exasperation making him sound harsher than he intended. 'You can be just like her if you want. You can be kind, and you can be clever, and you're pretty already. Although I expect you're more like Ultramarine than Leah to look at.'

This remark impressed his sister for some reason. She slowly turned her head and peeped out at him from the pillow. 'But we'll never really know, will we?' she said.

Someone outside the room called softly, 'Children, I have something for you!'

Ned opened the door and found Rhoda standing in the passage.

'Leah told me you'd been asking for – papers,' she said. 'And I thought you should have this. I suppose it belongs to your father but, well, he could never be

167

found.' She handed Ned another long envelope, this one very creased and stained. In fact it was so battered Ned wondered if the contents would scatter like dust the moment he let it into the light.

'It's your parents' marriage certificate,' Rhoda explained. 'I thought it might help. And this is for Nell, from her grandmother. She gave it to me today.' She placed a package in Ned's empty hand and went away without a backward glance.

Ned gave the small soft parcel to his sister and sat beside her on the bed. She carefully read aloud the message scrawled in long uneven characters on the white tissue paper. 'For my granddaughter, it says.' She turned hopefully to Ned. 'D'you think she had begun to like me after all?'

'Yes,' he said thoughtfully. 'I think she broke out of her dark days just in time to remember the way we had all been, once, before her troubles changed her. That's good, isn't it?'

Nell nodded slowly. She untied the string and folded back the tissue. On her knees lay a baby's dress creamed by sunshine and salt water, its hem and sleeves so feathery with soft lace it looked like thistledown. And where the baby's heart might have been there was an exquisite 'R' embroidered in the palest of pink silk.

'Whose is it?' Nell said wonderingly.

'Yours,' Ned told her.

'But R?' She pointed to the embroidered letter.

'She made it for you. You'll understand, I promise. Our grandmother wasn't angry through and through. She loved us, once, before things got so dark she couldn't see her books, and before she began to believe the kelpie had it in for her.'

Nell gazed at the tiny careful stitches, proof that her grandmother had once loved her. She held the little dress up to the light and, as she did so, something slipped through the folds and fell on to the floor: a neat brown box. The same shaky hand had written on the lid: 'For Both!'

Ned picked up the box and opened it. A girl smiled up at him from a small silver frame: she had a cloud of shining golden hair and eyes like the dark blue sea.

'Ultramarine,' Nell murmured, leaning close.

'You're like her,' Ned said.

'Am I?' she said gratefully.

They stared at the portrait for a long silent moment, then Ned propped the frame on his bedside table, where their strange, beautiful mother could watch them discover who they were.

'I want you to read this before we go any further,' Ned said. And he placed in Nell's hands the precious scrap of paper that would tell her her true name.

Nell unfolded the paper and read wonderingly. 'Rainbow. Is that me?'

'Yes. It's strange but I remember the word from long, long ago. I can hear myself calling it, only my voice is high like a baby. Perhaps your name was the first word I ever said.'

'But it's the word that Arion drew in the sand for me. I never thought that it could really be mine.'

'And mine is Albatross,' he told her.

'How did Arion know?' She gazed out at the sea, always there to mystify and delight her.

'Perhaps this will tell us.' Ned gingerly opened the envelope Rhoda had given to him. Though creased this paper was far more impressive than their birth certificates. It was long and thick and covered with names and dates and places. There was Marina McQueen and her father Alistair McQueen. And in a column beside it, Marina's husband – Albatross Rainbow Indigo Oyster Nightingale. His father and mother were unknown. 'He gave his names to us,' Ned murmured.

'It's like he wasn't a real person at all,' Nell remarked, 'but made up of birds and colours. Like the words in a spell.' She touched her string of shells, reminding herself that she believed in magic.

Perhaps it was this gesture that drove Ned to the little cupboard where he had hidden his own gift; the mirror that showed a different Ned, a boy who belonged to the sea. Ned was ready for him now. He was ready to be Albatross. He stood close to the window so that his features should be more truthfully revealed by the light that was left in the sky. Half-closing his eyes he searched for the sort of man he might become, scrutinizing the hairline, the chin and the eyebrows, shutting out the distraction of the still childish nose and cheeks. And a man appeared in the misty silver, with sea-green eyes and salt shining on his face in tiny crystals. 'I know who I am, Arion,' Ned told the smiling stranger. 'But now what?'

And Nell, who often saw things that others didn't, provided the answer. She brought the long sheet of paper to the window and pointed in turn to the letters that began each of her father's names. 'A and R and I and O and N,' she said looking at Ned for confirmation.

'Arion!' he exclaimed. 'You're clever, Nell. You've caught him!'

'She took the words out of the sky and the sea,' Nell declared, her joyful little smile awake again. 'The names of all the things she loved. She carved them into wooden beads and gave them to her baby.'

'Yes,' Ned replied. 'Our other grandmother. What shall we do now?' It was the first time in his life he had ever asked his sister for advice.

'Go and tell him,' she said, as though it would be

ridiculous to suppose any alternative was possible.

'It's nearly dark,' he reminded her, and like an echo, the sky tipped a golden cloud behind the towering cliffs. 'And suppose he doesn't want us to find out,' he added anxiously.

'Well, we have,' Nell said. 'Come on!' She bounded out of the room and down the stairs while Ned followed, cautiously slow.

Outside the living-room the hum of grave voices caused a hesitation in Nell's abandoned flight and she opened the door. When Ned reached the hall she was walking towards Leah.

'I'm sorry about the egg,' Nell said. 'I couldn't help it. It seemed so cruel. All those real eggs won't be laid now because the birds are dying and...' All at once she gave a long cry.

'What is it, Nell?' Leah took both her hands.

'My own bird died!' Nell sobbed. 'My painted warrior. But I had to pretend it flew away. I had to! I had to!' She fell into Leah's arms and Leah held her tight until the storm was over. Then stroking all the tears away, Leah said, 'I understand!'

The window of darkening sky beyond turned their two figures into a little island, and Ned remembered that they were on their way to the sea. 'We were going out,' he murmured apologetically.

'Where to?' Leah released Nell, frowning.

'To see our father,' Nell told her happily.

While Leah and Mark gazed at their children, uncomprehending, Ned saw the ghost of a smile touch Rhoda's lips. She knows, he thought, or has she only guessed?

'Who?' Leah said, turning to Mark for help with yet another bewildering problem.

'Didn't you guess?' Ned came forward with the paper meant for Arion. He held it up to Leah and

Mark, indicating the five special letters, now underlined by Nell.

'But, Ned, that doesn't mean...It could be a coincidence.'

'Our names,' he said. 'Our very, very peculiar names.'

'That does seem to indicate a connection.' Sensible Mark looked at his wife.

'He's in my face,' Ned persisted. 'Didn't you notice? You know me so well.'

'He's a grown man and – quite different,' she said stupidly.

And Ned suddenly realized that she was afraid for him. His true father had never yet revealed himself. Perhaps he wanted to remain disconnected and free of children always. But he had come to them, didn't that mean he wanted them?

'I think it's going to be all right,' he told Leah. 'He wanted us to find out but he's not around people very much and doesn't know how to tell them things.'

'I agree,' Rhoda spoke up, adding, 'but you'd better hurry.'

He was standing with his back to the sea, his white shirt startling as spray against the dark water. When he saw them he came to meet them, his bare feet carrying him fast over the silvery beach.

Ned held out the much-travelled marriage certificate. 'This belongs to you,' he said. 'It was our mother's too.'

Arion took the paper and walked away from them. He sat on the sand and gazed at the paper and then he looked out at the ocean.

They thought he had either forgotten them or didn't want to admit who they were but as they began to retreat, sad and unsure, he stopped them saying,

'Please stay a moment, children,' and he carefully buttoned the paper into his breast pocket.

They went to sit at either side of their father and, without a word, he put an arm round each of them and they sat together, very quietly, listening to the ocean and watching the great beautiful movements of the waves.

At last Ned had to break the spell and ask, 'Why didn't you tell us, right at the beginning, who you were?'

'I wasn't sure who you were,' Arion confessed.

'But the names you wrote in the sand,' Nell said. 'Weren't you testing us?'

'They are the names I carry in my head always,' he told her. 'And when Ned wrote Ultramarine without knowing who she was, I seemed to hear her calling for her children.'

'Why did you leave her?' Ned asked, trying hard to keep accusation from creeping into his voice.

'There was so much to do. There will always be work to do out there. She understood. And she knew that babies do not mix with danger. She was with me, though, when she took out her boat, saving the birds, releasing the seals from their plastic nets. We were an ocean apart and yet we were together.'

'But you must have been lonely,' Nell said.

'Of course,' Arion said fiercely. 'Sometimes, I thought I would go mad with only the sea to talk to.'

'Why didn't you come back for us?' Ned would not let go of the runaway fisherman.

'Ah!' his father sighed. 'I had a friend on the islands, an old man who is still there. He writes to me from time to time. He told me whose children you had become and because I was cowardly and unsure in all my relationships except one, I was happy that you would be the children of such a good man. I knew

Dorian, you see. By then I had become a true albatross, a wanderer who had to keep flying away from the truth, away from knowing that I would never see Ultramarine again. I loved your mother so much, I couldn't bear to go near the land for a long time after she died. A kelpie has a heart, and a kelpie's heart can break. When I heard of Dorian's tragedy I was helping to clean up one of the worst oil spills there had ever been; I couldn't leave. I am an expert on pollution, you see, but I am not even halfway to being a good father.'

'You are! You are!' Nell cried.

'We had three years together, didn't we?' Ned remembered the tentative A – the first letter of his name, carved in Arion's boat. 'We sailed round the world together, but I can't remember any of it. I wish you could tell me all the things we did.'

'One day – Albatross,' Arion smiled. 'We'll retrace our life with Ultramarine.'

'Can't we come with you now?' Ned asked. 'Just for a few days.'

'Later,' Arion told him. 'But not yet. In time you and Nell will be old enough to take on all the dangers of the sea with me. Just wait!'

'I don't want to wait,' Nell suddenly exclaimed. 'I want to start helping, right now!'

'Daughter,' Arion said with a reproving smile. 'Do as I tell you. Be good to Leah and Mark. Grow up and learn what you have to and one day you'll be a splendid companion on my boat.'

Ned watched his sister caught, as if by magic, and changed abruptly into a happy and obedient girl. And he knew that she was safe.

'Someone was there,' he murmured. 'Someone saved us when we were babies and fell into the sea. I thought that it was you!'

Arion stood up, slowly brushing the sand from his

arms. It was not easy to see his expression in the fading light. 'I was somewhere on the ocean,' he said. 'But it was the sea that saved you!'

'Why would it do that?' Ned, turning to look at his father, caught the glimmer of stars in the darkening sky behind him.

'Who knows if the ocean has a purpose,' Arion replied. 'I have lived with it all my life but it is still a mystery. Four days ago it brought me to your door. Just as the wind carries an albatross.' Ned felt the luminous sea-eyes burning into him. 'Does it worry you, Ned, to know that you are a little different from other human beings?'

Ned, searching for an answer, looked at the stars; they were further away in time than the day that he and the albatross had evolved from the same invisible breath on the surface of the new-born world. To the stars he and the birds, the dolphin and the seals were all one.

'No,' he said. 'It doesn't worry me because we are all the same, really.'

'We just look different,' said Nell who must have read his thoughts.

They felt the warmth of Arion's approval in the strong hands that began to lead them away from the sea.

'You will come back?' Nell asked, then disguising her doubts, 'Of course, you will.'

'Of course I will!' her father said.

As they approached the steps up to the town, the sun, in a playful bedtime mood, slipped between the western crags and illuminated the cliff behind their house. The narrow shaft of light caught someone on a red bicycle swerving down the cliff road, her coat sailing behind her like great grey wings. Rhoda had never seemed the right shape for a cyclist and now she looked positively dangerous. The large suitcase laced behind her threatened to leap off at the first corner; her hat blew away and her tumbling hair covered her face, but she didn't stop.

'You're going to have a passenger after all,' Ned observed. 'I hope you've got room for a bike!'

And Arion, watching the determined cyclist swooping towards him, gave way to a bout of such unrestrained and delighted laughter, the children couldn't help joining in.